LUCIFER

SPEED DATING WITH THE DENIZENS OF THE UNDERWORLD

BOOK ONE

GINA KINCADE & ERZABET BISHOP

NAUGHTY NIGHTS PRESS LLC • CANADA

Sale of this book without a front cover may be unauthorized. If this book is coverless, it may have been reported to the publisher as "unsold or destroyed" and neither the author nor the publisher may have received payment for it.

No part of this book may be adapted, stored, copied, reproduced or transmitted in any form or by any means, electronic or mechanical, including photocopying, recording, or by any information storage and retrieval system, without permission in writing from the publisher.

Thank you for respecting the hard work of this author.

Lucifer

Speed Dating with the Denizens of the Underworld

Book One

Copyright © 2022

Gina Kincade & Erzabet Bishop

ISBN: 978-1-77357-344-1

978-1-77357-345-8

Published by Naughty Nights Press LLC

Cover Art By King Cover Designs

Names, characters and incidents depicted in this book are products of the author's imagination or are used fictitiously. Any resemblance to actual events, locales, organizations, or persons, living or dead, is entirely coincidental and beyond the intent of the author.

LUCIFER

Only his fated mate could bring Lucifer to his knees...

Confirmed bachelor and legendary playboy, Lucifer Morningstar, is the cocky King of the Underworld. By day, he moonlights as the owner of the DeLux Cafe, and at night he controls evil supernatural beings in the underworld. One stroke of his whip makes immortal demons grovel and quake. With his faithful hellhound by his side, life couldn't be better.

That is, until he meets a delicious Detective and can't get her out of his mind. Lucifer is obsessed with chasing

LUCIFER

down his fated mate and making her his.

Detective Chloe Frost moved to LA four years ago to further her career. She's driven and good at her job. A white wolf shifter, she has a nose for these things. Being the best detective she can be is all she wants…even if she is lonely without her pack. Her true love is her profession. Who needs a man anyhow?

Despite her negative outlook on love, Chloe accepts her friend's suggestion to attend a speed dating mingle at the DeLux Cafe. Heidi swears it's just what Chloe needs. Her hopes aren't high, but a little fun-n-sexy-times won't hurt, right?

Lucifer is book one in the Speed Dating with the Denizens of the Underworld shared world, filled with devilish demons, sinful shifters, and more.

DEDICATION

For Mackenzie

*I'm so proud of you for breaking out
and becoming your true self.
May you live your best life every
single day!*

CHAPTER ONE

FAR BENEATH THE human world, Lucifer Morningstar, the ruler of the Underworld, sat on his throne feeling generally very pleased with himself. The last three days had brought a great deal of chaos to his home. There had been a great influx of new arrivals in Purgatory; new arrivals that needed taming. All of

LUCIFER

Lucifer's lesser demons had tried to get a handle on all of the new demons, but nothing seemed to be working. Finally, he decided that it was time for him to step in.

Why leave the job to the amateurs when it will take the professional under ten seconds?

That was why today when he'd gotten up, Lucifer had deviated from his usual schedule. As the ruler of the Underworld, he generally took things in quite a leisurely manner; he woke when he wanted to, slept when he felt like it, and demanded food when he got hungry. He did as he pleased, because there was no one else in Purgatory who was going to try and tell him otherwise.

Instead of sleeping in late, Lucifer

had risen early. He'd taken extra care in making sure his wings looked as sharp and as hellish as possible by washing them and even trimming off the tips to create new ones. Stretched out, they were twice as large as he was, which was a feat in itself. He flapped the inky black feathers a few times, noting that the reddish tinge to the tips reminded him of the crimson color of blood. He flashed a demonic smile at himself in the mirror inside of his castle, his eyes bright and glowing scarlet. Turning on his heel, he charged over to the window, stepping off the sill and soaring into the smoky Purgatory sky.

As he soared high above his domain, he surveyed the chaos down below. The freshly minted demons hadn't yet gained

LUCIFER

control of their powers. Many of them were teleporting here, there, and everywhere, and it was all the Daemonium Guard—legions that protect Underworld's borders—could do to try and stop them for long enough to teach them. Other new demons were getting into scrapes, shooting fire, and trying to kill each other. And still other demons were trying to destroy everything that surrounded them on the ground, which proved to be far more difficult than many of them thought. Each blast they provided that was directed toward any sort of structure was immediately repelled and shot back at them. They didn't seem to learn, however, and so they just kept injuring themselves more and more.

GINA KINCADE & ERZABET BISHOP

Lucifer did another lap around the chaotic scene below him, just to make sure that he wasn't missing anything, and then he chose his spot to land—right in the middle of everything. He slammed down onto the ground, his fist hitting the earth at the same time his feet and one knee did. Thunder rumbled through the ground and lightning cascaded through the sky. The demons immediately shut up and everything stopped, the new, abrupt silence almost deafening. Lucifer growled menacingly as he stood. He could feel the heat in his eyes and knew they were full on crimson as he looked out over the silent crowd.

"You were brought here," he seethed, "because you were chosen. You all have something within you that we see as

LUCIFER

potential. This potential could make you become a great demon groomed properly by the Daemonium Guard. Or it could destroy you if you insist on continuing to act like the imbeciles that you are. Now, are you going to obey me, or are you going to cause mayhem?"

The silence continued for a few moments after he finished speaking, each demon looking from one to the other as if asking 'what the hell, who is this dude?' This did not please Lucifer. Quite the opposite, in fact. He expected everyone under him to obey his every command. When he said fly, they were to say how high. When he was displeased, they were to fix it. And when he told them to obey him, they were to do so. His felt his blood heat at this atrocious display.

Suddenly, there was a great growl from the crowd and pure chaos broke out once more, only now it was worse. All of the new demons were charging directly toward him at lightning speed. Contrary to what it may have seemed, Lucifer hoped this was what would happen. He chucked inwardly, taking a perverse pleasure in the events about to unfold.

These fools.

Don't they know what I'm capable of?

Don't they know that I am not to be trifled with?

If they think that they are going to overtake me... they have another thing coming to them.

Lucifer didn't flinch, move, or bat an

eye. He simply closed his eyes, concentrated on his inner power for not longer than a millisecond, and then with a flick of his wrist power rushed out of him. Akin to a supersonic sound wave, it lay waste to all of the rebellious new demons in its path. The Daemonium Guard, however, remained untouched. That was a part of Lucifer's ultimate power: he could choose exactly who he hurt and how much. He finally opened his eyes as all of the new demons went flying backward, madly clawing at the air, trying to stop themselves. They all fell with a thunderous clap at the same time, and then... the blessed silence resumed.

Lucifer crossed his arms in front of him and looked out at the carnage he had created. The new demons were not dead, of course, but they didn't know this. He laughed, a great, deep outward laugh that had maniacal beginnings. The new demons eventually began struggling to get up, looking like a bunch of drunk teenagers who were waking up from a bad trip. When they had all stumbled roughly to their feet, Lucifer began talking again.

"If any of you would like to test me again, please, be my guest," he stated firmly. "Otherwise, I would suggest that you obey the Daemonium Guard General. If you do not, you will be forced to face my wrath again... only next time it will be even worse."

No demon said anything or made any moves in response to what Lucifer had

LUCIFER

said.

My work here is done.

Lucifer shot into the sky and flew back to his castle. He blasted in through the window and came to a stop at the top of a dais. Turning on his heel, he took his place on his throne, feeling pleased with himself. He knew he was the best ruler Purgatory had ever seen, but even he hadn't thought he was *that* good. The thought made a chuckle slip from his lips.

He threw a leg over the side of his chair and leaned back, pondering how he was going to pass the rest of his day—would he take a stroll throughout the castle to ensure that all of his repairs were being done correctly? Would he lie in bed and fantasize about all of the women up on earth who he was going to meet up with at the Underworld Cafe and seduce when he returned to his double life? Or would he—

His cell phone rang, interrupting his musing. He had entirely forgotten he even had one of the blasted contraptions. He had been so against getting one. In his mind, if anyone wanted to contact him they would find a way that didn't involve speaking on the phone.

Lucifer begrudgingly grabbed it off of his side table, swiped his thumb across the green button, and put the phone to his ear.

"What?" he barked into it.

"Ooooh, someone doesn't sound happy today," the other voice purred

LUCIFER

from the other end. "Is it my fault, Lucifer? You must have seen my name on the call display and thought 'this means trouble.'"

Lucifer let out a low chuckle. "Hello, Aphrodite. Couldn't resist me for too long, now could you?"

"Resist you?" Aphrodite responded. "More like require you."

Lucifer drummed his fingers on the armrest of his throne. "I always love to be wanted more than I know I am. And what do you require me for today, my goddess of love? Is it something that requires you having me all to yourself?"

Aphrodite laughed sarcastically. "If it were, would it get you to come back to the cafe faster?"

"Maybe," Lucifer growled. "You know

how I like it when you want me like that."

Now, Aphrodite laughed uproariously. "Oh, Lucifer. Haven't you learned? I don't require your services of that variety anymore. I don't feed off of seduction, and I've told you that many times. Now, I get my fix from the love of the people who I set up here at the cafe."

Lucifer rolled his eyes. "When are you going to drop that act, Aphie? I know you want me, you know you want me… let's cut to the chase."

"You want to cut to the chase, do you?" Aphrodite asked, amused. "All right. What I require you for is a shift at the cafe. Adam quit on me again, and he says that it's for good this time. He and Eve are finalizing their divorce in a few days and according to him, he can't stand the sight of her for a minute longer. Ta da."

"Wait," Lucifer said, sitting up straighter in his throne. "You called me in the middle of one of the best days I've had in a long time down here to ask me to come up to earth to cover a shift at the cafe for Adam? That's what this is about?"

"That's what this is about," Aphrodite repeated to him. "And if you don't like it, why don't you just hand over your ownership rights to both the DeLux Cafe and the Underworld Cafe. Then you don't ever have to hear from me again."

Lucifer sighed and rubbed the ends of his wings. "You saucy little minx. You know I'm never going to give that up.

Where else in either of our worlds is there a cafe on both sides of the veil? Where else would everyone like us go to mix and mingle?"

"If you let me own this place it will still exist, Lucifer," Aphrodite said smartly. "It'll just have a better owner and be run tighter!"

Lucifer laughed out loud. "You wish. All right. I'm going to tie up a few loose ends here and then I'll be up. Does that please you enough?"

"Better than you used to please me," Aphrodite snarked. "Get here ASAP. I'm not waiting on you for hours like I did the last time."

Lucifer punched the red button on the phone, disconnecting the call. He glanced around the room and then out the window, a sigh leaving his lips. It looked so much less appealing outside now that he actually had to go somewhere. But he supposed there was nothing else he could do, and so he collected his human clothes and began making his way up to earth.

CHAPTER TWO

SPECIAL AGENT CHLOE Frost's neck was beginning to twinge. She had been looking at the abstract art in the corner of the victim's apartment for far too long, but she couldn't take her eyes off of it. It was unlike anything she had seen before, and that was saying something. Chloe had been with the department for

LUCIFER

sixteen years. She had worked cases that had involved just about everything. She'd caught a serial killer posing as his dead girlfriend who systematically killed everyone who he thought had some impact on her decision to take her own life. She'd worked a manslaughter case where a guy had been killed by his roommate's exploding Soda Stream when they tried to carbonate rubidium. And then there had been that time she'd discovered the weapon that a stay-at-home dad had used to bludgeon his wife was a leg of lamb he had been trying to serve to his children for dinner.

"Didn't your mother ever tell you that if you kept your neck like that for too long it would stay like that?" came a voice from behind Chloe.

GINA KINCADE & ERZABET BISHOP

She snapped out of her daze and whipped her head back upright a little too quickly, causing it to ache. She rubbed it as she turned around to give her partner, Detective Gloria Diaz, a sarcastic smile.

"Then you must have contorted your face into all kinds of ugly shapes to get it to look that hideous," Chloe spat back at her. The two women stared each other down for ten seconds, and then they both laughed.

"That was pretty good, you're learning fast," Diaz said, patting Chloe on the back. She then twisted her neck the same way that Chloe had and squinted her eyes as she, too, analyzed the art.

"What do you think?" Chloe asked her. "It looks like someone took the

LUCIFER

insides of one of the millions of rotting lunch containers inside of Venus' locker and hucked it onto a canvas."

Diaz chuckled and crossed her arms, shaking her head. "Nah, man, not even Venus could have produced something that... unnatural looking."

Diaz turned around and shouted over to the tall, nerdy looking guy on the other side of the room who was right in the middle of delicately putting a shard of glass in an evidence bag. "Hey, Toombs, get over here and give us some sort of an artsy explanation for this."

Wallace Toombs dropped the shard of glass he had been working so hard on when he heard Diaz yelling at him. Chloe could see the frustration rise and fall on his face, and then he came over to stand beside her partner. He craned his neck forward and squinted at the art just as the rest of them had. After a minute, he rolled his eyes, put on a new pair of gloves, and turned each of the three paintings to the right one rotation. When he did that, all three could clearly see that they were portraits of a twisted looking turtle, a drooping starfish, and palm tree that looked like it had seen better days.

"Yes, piece requires a great deal of artistic interpretation," Toombs said sarcastically. "If I were a betting man, I'd say that this piece was purchased in a far off land sometimes referred to as 'Mexico.'"

"You're telling me that I just spent the last ten minutes at a crime scene analyzing a vacation painting?" Chloe asked dryly.

"It certainly seems that way," Toombs replied. "But don't be too hard on yourself. I hear that art like this fascinates minds like yours for *hours* on end."

Chloe narrowed her eyes, barely suppressing the growl that threatened to come from her wolf. "What do you mean, minds like mine?"

Toombs shrugged. "Oh, don't take it so personally, Queen Elsa of the Frost. What are you going to do, strangle me with your majestic hair? You're too small to do much damage otherwise and I don't think you're in good enough shape to come running after me, right?"

Chloe's inner wolf growled, the sound

bubbling up her throat. She had to stop herself; she couldn't go shifting right here and now. No one at the LAPD knew about her dual-nature, and she wasn't about to show them over a lousy derogatory comment from the likes of Toombs. She could feel her wolf's claws dying to come out through her nails, pressing on the underside of the nail bed, and her fur bristled beneath her skin. The downy white hairs on her arms that were the same color and silky softness as her fur began to quiver in anticipation of her shift. Her elegant white wolf form was ready to take over and tear the man limb from limb at any second.

Down girl.

She shook her long, silvery-white

mane of hair out of her face, and shushed her wolf, trying to convince it not to turn skin into fur. Flashing her piercing, icy blue eyes at Toombs, she hoped the jerk felt like he'd been stabbed by an icicle.

"What did you just say to her?" Diaz asked, stepping in front of her. "That is classic workplace harassment, Toombs, and if you don't get yourself out of this room in the next three seconds, you're going to have a department mandated suspension on your hands."

Toombs sighed and crossed his arms in front of him. "It was a joke, Diaz. Can't you women take a joke? God. Fine, I'll go."

With that, Toombs turned around and left the room. Chloe was still shaking, her wolf scratching at her skin, begging her to let her at him. She resisted the almost undeniable pressing urge to chuff, snort, and growl her way into her animal form, but the desire to shift remained strong. She needed to get out of there and blow off some steam. She needed to run. It'd been way too long and her wolf needed the release as much as she did.

Diaz stepped in front of her and looked into her eyes. "Frost? You okay?"

Chloe nodded quickly. "Thank you for saying that. I just need to go get some fresh air, I'll be right back." She darted out of Diaz's sight so fast and out of the apartment complex even faster.

She let the outer door slam behind her and ran for the edge of the property.

LUCIFER

When she was finally out in the brisk night air, and out of sight of anyone else, she gave into the urge to shift. Letting her wolf have her head, she felt the prickling sensation as fur emerged from beneath her skin. Her hands and feet snapped and cracked as they shifted into four legs and paws. Her face elongated into a fuzzy snout and she let out a deep, guttural snarl. Although she may have been short, curvy and humble looking in her human form, she was a force to be reckoned with in her animal form.

She took off like a jet into the night, running to all of the shadowy places where she knew she wouldn't be seen. It felt so good to feel the wind in her fur and get out all of the anger she felt toward Toombs.

I can't believe he would say something like that to me.

What a horrible, disgusting thing to say to another person.

How in the hell did he know I'm self-conscious about my height, weight and my hair?

Do I really project that so outwardly?

As Chloe ran in her white wolf form, she began to feel so much better. After about five minutes of feeling her footpads hitting the earth, stretching powerful legs until they ached, Chloe felt ready to go back to the crime scene. She quickly wound her way back to the apartment complex where the victim had been found, and then went down a dark alley to shift back into her human form.

LUCIFER

Just as quickly as it had appeared, her fur disappeared beneath her skin, her paws turned back into her legs and arms, her white hair re-emerged from the top of her head, and her face returned to normal. She was ready to go back inside.

As she re-entered the apartment, no one took any notice of her except for Detective Diaz, who came right over to her.

"Hey, you sure you're okay?" Diaz asked, genuinely concerned. "You booked it out of here pretty quickly… and you've got mud on your face now?"

Chloe put her hand to her face and quickly wiped the streak of mud away. "Yeah, I'm fine, totally fine. Let's look at this body and forget all about Toombs, okay?"

Chloe bent down and took a closer look at the carpet that the body was lying on. There were two indentations in the carpet right by his shoulder, but there was also one on one side of his hip. Chloe craned her neck over the other side of the body and saw that there was an identical indentation on the other side. That got her train of thought chugging at a good clip.

"I'm heading to the bathroom," she said as she got up and walked into the bathroom just off the living room. All of the victim's bathroom items were laid out on the counter in a very organized manner. He seemed to have bought up every organizing box that the dollar store had to offer. The stuff was obviously cheap, but it made her like the victim just a little more. He was obviously trying... or rather, he had obviously tried.

"You seem to have an idea of something that happened here," Diaz prompted her, following in behind her. She sat on the closed toilet seat and began looking at the evidence around it. "What are you seeing that I'm not?"

"I don't know yet," Chloe replied, gingerly opening the medicine cabinet door with her gloved finger. Inside, it was fairly empty except for one container of hydrocortisone cream and a bottle of no name multi vitamins. The exact same no name brand vitamin that she had in her own medicine cabinet, actually, and she just had a slightly different type of medicated cream. Her brow furrowed. "Have you noticed anything helpful yet?"

Diaz was now completely doubled over, analyzing the victim's floor. "Not a thing. This guy seems to have led a pretty self-contained life. I can't imagine who would want to kill him."

Chloe bagged the cream and the vitamins, and then scowled at her partner. Diaz pointed at something. "Look," she said.

Chloe bent down to see numerous small circular indentations in the crappy laminate flooring covering the bathroom. "Heels," she said quietly, and Diaz nodded.

"But no toothbrush, no drawer, not even a sign of a date. Did you see what he was wearing? I don't think even a guy his age would be caught dead in that outfit in front of a woman." Diaz chuckled. "Although, I suppose that's exactly what happened."

Chloe laughed, and then the two women returned to the living room. When she saw the body, she saw what Diaz meant. The victim wore a beige wool sweater that looked very moth-eaten and ratty. His sweatpants had stains on them and the drawstring seemed to be barely clinging to his waist.

"Do you think..." Chloe started, walking toward the body. A flash of something in the carpet caught her eye.

There.

What is that?

Something shiny glimmered in the carpet to the right of the victim's head.

GINA KINCADE & ERZABET BISHOP

"What'd you see?" Diaz asked, following her.

As Chloe walked toward the object that had grabbed her attention, she noticed that there were takeout containers littering the kitchen counter. She recognized almost all of them—the plain white Styrofoam with the yellow and green sticker was from the House of Joyful Chinese food place, the aluminum container with the white lid and the highlighter yellow writing on the top was from Gary's Place, and there were two pizza boxes from San Marco's. Chloe was beginning to feel more and more like she was walking around in her own home, and she didn't like it.

"Frost?" Diaz asked, pulling her out of her thoughts. Chloe snapped her attention back to her partner, and then continued walking.

"Yeah, sorry," Chloe said distractedly as she bent down to get a better look at the gem nestled in the carpet. It looked very plastic and very fake, which was exactly what Chloe had been expecting. She pried a pair of needle-nose tweezers out of her crime scene kit and extracted the jewel from the carpet. She held it up for Diaz to see. When she got one look at it, she crossed her arms in front of her and rolled her eyes.

"You thinking what I'm thinking?" Diaz asked, sounding both disappointed an annoyed.

Chloe nodded. She looked down at the victim's vacant face and gave him a sad smile. "I think mister here just wanted to have a good time. He found a 'professional' that he liked, but she might have accidentally gone a little too far with the choking. Do you think she at least got paid?"

Diaz pointed to the victim's pocket, and Chloe noted that it had the bulge of a wallet in it. Chloe extracted it with her gloved hands, opened it and saw that there was a wad of money inside of it.

"That's a shame," Diaz said, walking up behind her. "Those girls work too hard to not get paid when they just accidentally kill a guy. I'll bet he was loving it right up until he died; he would have given her a great tip. Cases like these make me not want to follow up with the investigation. It was an accident, she didn't mean to do it, and he was probably miserable anyway."

Chloe whipped around to face her partner. "What makes you say that?" she asked a little too defensively.

Diaz gave her a strange look. "Uhhh, have you seen this place? All the decor is varying shades of beige, he ordered out every night, all of his things look so cheap and sad... Wouldn't you be miserable if this was you?"

"No," Chloe snapped back quickly. "I think our vic was a smart guy. He spent money on the things that he really loved, like that cabinet full of collector Lord of the Rings things in the corner, or the Orc Sword in his cabinet. Everything else was purely functional, and maybe that was the way he liked it. And it's really hard to cook for just one person.

GINA KINCADE & ERZABET BISHOP

Did you ever try making a lasagna for yourself when you were on your own? You have to eat it meal after meal for like weeks to finish it all."

When Chloe finished speaking, she knew that she had sounded oddly protective of the vic, but there wasn't much she could do about that now. The truth was, she felt like her and the victim weren't that different; they led quiet, unassuming lives that didn't involve many other people, and maybe he got a little too into his work like she did. But as she looked at him lying there on the carpet, having been killed by a sex worker who accidentally smothered him to death, it made her realize something: both she and this man were very, very lonely.

LUCIFER

Diaz started laughing at her. "Geesh, Frost, you sound like you want to marry this guy. But if this is your type, I'm going to be a bit surprised. I thought you would have liked guys who were... a little younger and a little less..."

"Dead?" Chloe finished for her.

"No. Frumpy," she said, chuckling, and Chloe joined her. "But come to think of it, I've never seen you with a guy around the station. When was the last time you went on a date?"

Chloe knew that she needed to get out of this conversation quickly, otherwise she was going to be the laughing stock of their department. "I uh... " She grabbed for her phone, pretending she felt the vibration of an incoming call. "Oh, Heidi is calling me. I have to take this. Sorry."

She put her phone to her ear and began to have a conversation with her best friend, who most certainly hadn't called her. As she walked away from Diaz and continued faking the discussion with her friend on the phone, Chloe came to a realization: she didn't want to end up like the poor man here. His unfortunate ending spooked her, made her take a second look at her own mundane and boring life. She wanted to get out and meet people, even if they weren't the right people right away. She needed something outside of work, some sort of actual social life. She decided that as soon as she left here tonight, she was going to call up Heidi for real and ask her to hook her up with someone. She

LUCIFER

hoped that would make some sort of small difference, otherwise she was going to have to take matters into her own hands.

CHAPTER THREE

WHEN CHLOE FINISHED her shift that evening, she immediately wanted to go home and get into her usual routine—order up some food, eat it while sitting on the couch watching some Jeopardy, and then play her favorite online RPG game. It was called 'WolfMoon', which she originally thought was incredibly

LUCIFER

cheesy, but outside of the name, she absolutely loved it. She had created, unsurprisingly, a white wolf character named Remi that she played as. The graphics were so advanced that when she was playing, it really felt as though she had stepped into another world. She loved getting lost in the adventures, tuning out real life and becoming completely absorbed in the game for hours.

Of course, the fact that her packmate, Randall Graves, had been the brilliant mind to create the game and make a cool billion or so on the venture didn't have any bearing on her love for the game. Okay, well maybe a little bit, if she were honest. She'd always had a secret childhood crush on the intelligent member of her Alpha's Wolf Guard.

Much of the decoration in her bedroom was from the game, and she especially treasured the 3D model of Remi that she'd had made by a seller on Etsy. It was proudly displayed on her table in the front hall; practically the first thing that anyone saw when they came in.

Tonight, though, Chloe thought she should break with tradition, especially after the similarities she'd noted between herself and the victim tonight. The problem was, though, Chloe didn't really know what else to do this evening. She could call up Heidi and start telling her about her desire to start dating again, but that would probably get Heidi overly excited, and she wasn't sure if she had enough energy in her to deal with that. She could go for a nice drive down the 1, maybe all the way down to Newport Beach. That was one of her favorite drives in the world, but she'd done it so many times...

Ugh.

She needed something new and exciting to shake herself out of this rut. But before she decided to make any big decisions like that, she did have to go down to evidence and see if they'd processed the gun that had been dredged out of the waterway where one of her other victims had been found. She shut off her desk light, collected up her things and took the elevator down to evidence.

When the doors opened, Chloe's

spirits immediately picked up because the heavenly face of Mackenzie Wylde was smiling back at her.

"Chloe!" Mackenzie cried, throwing up her arms with delight. "It's been so long since you've come to visit me, what has it been, like, three days?"

"Three days is long enough for me, Mackenzie," she said to her. "How've you been, what's new?"

"Well, the most exciting thing that's gone on around here is that I got a new wireless mouse, so how about you tell me what's going on up top? There's got to be something more exciting than wireless mice happening up there," Mackenzie said, taking a long swig of her coffee.

Chloe chuckled and pulled up a chair

on the other side of Mackenzie's desk. "Hey, don't belittle your wireless mouse, it took me six months to get the department to give me a new desk chair. I had a letter from my physiotherapist and everything! It was like pulling teeth, honestly."

"Yeah, yeah, I guess I should be celebrating my small victories," Mackenzie said. "Come on, don't hold back, I heard you got called out on a potential homicide tonight. What happened?"

Chloe put her feet up on Mackenzie's desk and leaned back in her chair. "I'll tell you, Mackenzie, it was one of the saddest cases I've ever been to. Older guy, lived alone, death by strangulation, and Diaz and I think that it might have been a... you know... pleasurable kind of strangulation that went a bit too far."

Mackenzie arched her eyebrow and whistled. "Wow. I wonder if I know the girl who did it, I've got a bunch of friends who know ladies in that line of work. Any chance you might know what type of shoe the killer was wearing?"

Chloe wiggled her head from side-to-side as if to say 'so-so.' "The best I can give you is that they're probably stilettos."

"Did the apartment smell like anything when you came in?" Mackenzie asked, obviously very engaged in this mystery now.

Chloe thought for a moment, and then did recall smelling something when she first came in. "Peppermint. But not

LUCIFER

perfume... sort of medicinal."

Mackenzie grimaced and made a sound of displeasure. "I don't like the sounds of that. My buddy Octavia has a friend who goes by Crystal Candy who always wears bright pink stilettos and has this peppermint rub that she uses for her chronic migraines. I really hope she hasn't gotten caught up in any of that nasty business."

"I hope not too, but even if she did, we'd probably be able to get her off pretty easy if it turns out it was a complete accident," Chloe responded, taking her feet off the table and looking at Mackenzie earnestly.

Mackenzie chuckled. "You'd be able to get her off pretty easy, eh? I thought that was supposed to be her job!"

Chloe laughed, and then became more serious. "Could you see if Octavia has any contact info for Crystal? I'll reach out to her and tell her what you told me. I'm sure she's not involved, but it's better to cover all my bases."

Mackenzie nodded and pulled out her phone. "I'll text her right now."

After Mackenzie had messaged Octavia, she gave Chloe a hard look. "Now tell me, I know there's some other reason why you came down to visit me, but I can tell something is on your mind. What's up?"

Chloe rolled her eyes and crossed her arms. "You know me better than I know myself, Mackenzie. It's nothing major, really. It's just that when we were at the victim's apartment tonight I... I noticed some similarities between the two of us. It's silly, really." She felt heat stain her cheeks.

Mackenzie looked perplexed. "Was it that you're both dead inside?"

Chloe had to chuckle. "No, it was that he and I both lead quiet, unassuming lives, and I don't want to end up like he did."

Mackenzie immediately dropped her joking and schooled her features to imply she took what Chloe was saying seriously. She leaned forward at her desk and placed her clasped hands atop the table. "I'm sorry to hear you're feeling that way, Chloe. It's a downright rotten feeling, and I don't want to reassure you right out of the gate, but you're not going to end up like that guy.

For one thing, I wouldn't let you hire a girl like Crystal. I'd get you someone much better than her."

Chloe laughed out loud. She and Mackenzie had been work friends since the very beginning. In fact, Mackenzie was probably one of her first friends in the department. She remembered the first day she came down to evidence looking for Mackenzie because someone had told her to come down and grab 'him'. Chloe was so nervous back then that when she walked up to the glass she was practically shaking.

"Excuse me," Chloe had said quietly, "I'm looking for Mackenzie Wylde? Someone asked me to come down and get him."

Mackenzie had rolled her eyes. "It

LUCIFER

was Spencer, wasn't it? No matter how many talks he's been given by the department, he won't stop calling me 'him' and 'he'. You can tell him that until he starts respecting my pronouns, he won't be getting any favors from me."

Chloe had looked back at Mackenzie with wide eyes. "I... I'm so sorry. What are your pronouns?"

Mackenzie had looked taken aback, as though she didn't get that response too often. "Uh... she/her, if you wouldn't mind. What's yours? And what's your name?"

"'She,'" Chloe had answered, flashing a smile and becoming more at ease around Mackenzie. "I'm Chloe Frost. I just started here."

Mackenzie nodded her head,

impressed. "Sweet. Frost suits you with hair like that. You look like you could braid that hair together and make yourself a mighty fine tethering rope."

Chloe had laughed out loud. "I'll tell Detective Spencer what you said. And... He's a schmuck for not respecting how you'd like to be addressed. I haven't liked him from the moment I met him."

With that, Mackenzie had smiled broadly at her, and they'd been close ever since. They were such good friends, in fact, that Chloe had even thought about revealing her shifting identity to her, but that would still be a little while yet. She was so cautious about revealing her true identity to anyone because it came with such a great risk.

Back in the present, Chloe responded

LUCIFER

to Mackenzie's joke. "That's very kind of you, but I really am worried that I'm becoming too stuck in my 'safe' ways. I liked going to that Halloween party you had, but I haven't done anything like that since then."

Mackenzie stared at her, dumbfounded. "You... you haven't done anything as 'exciting' as my timid little Halloween party that was... nine months ago? Oh my god. Okay, this situation is a lot more dire than I thought!"

Chloe nodded. "Right? I've been thinking about calling up Heidi and seeing if she had any ideas of how I could shake things up, but if you can think of anything, please, go ahead!"

Mackenzie looked off in the distance and smiled happily. "Mmmm, Heidi.

Never met a girl with hair as dark or a spirit as enchanting as hers. She's terrific, and judging by what you've told me about her, she's sure to have something up her sleeve to get you out of your funk. I just wish that she wasn't married to that emo punk. He's a real downer."

Heidi's hair was as magically dark as Mackenzie was describing it to be because she was a midnight wolf shifter, similar to Chloe. They both had almost identical shifter tendencies, and they'd been friends forever. They went back so far that Chloe could hardly even remember how she'd met Heidi.

Mackenzie was describing Heidi's husband, Dave, as an 'emo' because to humans, that was what Dave looked

LUCIFER

like. The man dressed all in black, had long, dark stringy hair, and his eyes naturally had big dark circles underneath them because in his non-human form, Dave was a demon. When Chloe had initially met him, she had been very hesitant about her best friend dating a demon, but she quickly warmed to him. He was, by far, the nicest demon she'd ever met, and he treated Heidi like a queen. She felt nothing but happiness now for her friend.

"Oh, he's not that bad," Chloe said, sticking up for him. "He's not very good in crowds, which is the only place you've ever seen him. I'll bring you over to their place with me sometime and you'll see how nice he really is."

Mackenzie arched an eyebrow and

looked at her skeptically. "Uh huh. Sure. I bet he's a barrel of laughs when you get him alone. But, anyway. I think that's a great idea. Heidi is bound to know someone who'd be the perfect match for you. Hasn't she tried setting you up with someone before?"

Chloe nodded. "You don't remember that one? Library Steve?"

Mackenzie audibly groaned. "Oh, no! I can't believe I forgot about Library Steve!"

The man they were referring to had been a distant relative of Heidi's who she'd set Chloe up with ages ago. They'd met at a pretty nice bar in the west end, but as soon as they'd sat down together, Library Steve had talked non-stop about the Dewey Decimal system. Chloe had tried to interject a number of times, but Library Steve just... went for it. Needless to say, she never called him for a second date.

"What if it's as bad as Library Steve?" Chloe whined.

"Then you call me from the bathroom and I come get you. I don't know why you didn't do that last time. I would have come in there with sirens a-blazing and gotten you out in under five seconds flat," Mackenzie told her, emphasizing her point with a loud smack of her palms together.

Chloe laughed heartily, and then brought up the case she had initially wanted to discuss with Mackenzie. Unfortunately, there weren't any more updates for her, so she reluctantly said goodbye to her friend and hurried along home.

She could only hope Heidi was her best bet for finding someone to get her out of this funk… as long as it wasn't Library Steve.

CHAPTER FOUR

"YOU HAVE TO be kidding me," Heidi replied, sitting across from her two days later at the Bejewels Lunch Bar. "The guy was killed by a… professional?"

"Shhh," Chloe hissed, leaning in toward her best friend. "If you say that too much louder the hipster couple at the table next to us will think we're discussing a hit man!"

Heidi laughed as she popped another piece of sushi in her mouth. The lunch bar was already packed, even though it was only eleven am, but it made sense. Bejewels was *the* spot to come for hip young professionals like themselves because the head chef, Lucy Karduak, had just been crowned Top Chef on America's Culinary Cook-off. Chloe thought that the name of the show was pretty stupid, considering it contained both the words 'culinary' and 'cook' when one could have sufficed. But no one else besides her seemed to be bothered by that. In fact, ten million people country-wide had tuned into the finale, most of them being from LA, and even more of them were already fans of

GINA KINCADE & ERZABET BISHOP

Lucy's.

When she won, the restaurant introduced her famous 'I Love Lucy Sushi' to everyone who hadn't already loved her before. A recipe so secret that it didn't even have the ingredients listed on the menu, which seemed to enrage some customers, but utterly delighted others.

Heidi ate one of said famous sushi burritos right now and seemed to be savoring it like it was the last meal she was ever going to have, if her moans and groans were any indication. Chloe, meanwhile, had decided to take a risk and try the 'Dizzy Desi', which was a basically a melt-in-your-mouth-delicious western omelet between two slices of sourdough bread that had been toasted to perfection. The omelet contained shallots, green onions, shrimp... and a whole bunch of other stuff that Chloe couldn't remember. Whatever those ingredients were didn't really matter; it was heavenly.

To go along with the 'I Love Lucy' theme of the food, the lunch bar was made up to look like a futuristic 1950's diner. There were the classic red vinyl booths and beige laminated tables, and then there was a line of bar stools covered in the same vinyl along the bar. The floor, however, looked like it had been ripped off of a spaceship. It had pieces of multicolored glitter embedded in it. When they reflected the overhead lights, it made it look like there were tiny lasers shooting at you every time you walked across the restaurant. Hanging from the ceiling were abstract pieces of art that had been made with broken records, and Lucy and Desi's faces were plastered all over the establishment. When you went to the bathroom, Technicolor Lucille Ball grinned back at you from the stall door. When you opened the menu, a Desi Arnaz cut out of holographic paper glittered back at you as you moved the page back and forth in the light. And now, as the two young women sat at the table, Chloe was having a hard time keeping her gaze off of the I Love Lucy reruns that were constantly playing on the TV's overhead.

"Oh, right," Heidi said, her voice down to an acceptable level of quietness and disappointment dripping in her tone. "I forgot there was more than one type of 'professional'." Heidi adjusted in her seat, giving Chloe a glimpse of her big, pregnant belly poking out from beneath the table.

"And when someone dies, it usually involves the other type," Chloe replied, not taking her gaze off the television. It was one of her favorite episodes; Lucy was trying to sell 'vegemeatavitamin.' Had she been back at her apartment right now, Chloe would have been rolling on the floor from laughing so hard.

"So what was it about that case that made you want to call me and ask me to set you up with someone—which, by the way, I am oh-so-happy to do?" Heidi asked, flashing a Cheshire-cat grin at her friend.

GINA KINCADE & ERZABET BISHOP

Chloe sighed and turned to face Heidi, her lips turning down at the corners. "It's just... There were a lot of things about his apartment that reminded me of myself, and it made me really... sad. I know I don't need a man to 'shake up' my life or anything, but I thought it might be a good place to start."

Heidi gleefully clapped her hands. "I think it's the perfect place to start! Let me pull out my contacts and see who I might be able to interest you in..." Heidi pushed her plate to the side, and it hurt Chloe just a little to see the future mama hadn't yet finished her sushi burrito.

The I Love Lucy Sushi burrito was always the best right when it was first served, and Chloe knew that by putting it to the side, Heidi was missing out on an explosion of flavor. However, she didn't want to tell her friend how to eat, so she swallowed her words and concentrated really hard on not allowing her gaze to drift back to the television.

Heidi pulled out her phone and put her elbows up on the table so that her screen was right in front of her face. "Okay, let's see... Hmmm, I don't think you'd be into Yuri, he's a shifter too, but he changes into a Kamchatka brown bear and I don't think you'd like that."

"Why not?" Chloe asked, suddenly intrigued. "I like bear shifters. They're usually very warm, cuddly... basically big teddy bears themselves."

Heidi widened her eyes and shook her head from side to side. "Absolutely not this one. He's more... tear you limb from limb kind of a bear than a big snuggly bear."

Chloe grimaced. "Oh. Good call, then. What else have you got?"

Heidi continued scrolling through her phone, making various 'thinking' faces and mumbling names to herself. "Ummmm... how do you feel about leprechauns?"

"As in Irish guys?" Chloe asked. "I haven't had great experiences with them in the past, but that doesn't mean—"

"No, I literally mean a leprechaun," Heidi said, turning her phone around so that Chloe could see who she was talking about. The person's name was Seamus O'Malley, and his icon was a very small man standing next to a very

LUCIFER

large pot of gold.

Chloe shrugged. "I mean, I'm not against it?"

Heidi nodded appreciatively, and then took one last scroll through her phone. But then, she froze with her finger against her screen and stared at Chloe.

"Wait. What am I doing? What's the date today?" she asked her.

Chloe pulled out her own phone and double checked. "The fifteenth?"

Heidi suddenly beamed from ear to ear. "What am I saying? You shouldn't go out with any of these guys. You need to go to the DeLux Cafe!" She dropped her phone into her purse where it sat on the floor, clearly figuring the solution had been decided.

The young homicide detective flashed

Heidi a doubtful look. "The place where you met Dave? I thought you said that I wouldn't like a place like that. In your words 'You'd hate it. It's dark, seedy, and moody... but that's why I loved it!'"

Heidi shook her head. "I don't mean just go there for a drink, you have to go there for their speed dating night! It's happening this month on the seventeenth, so this works out perfectly!"

The moment Chloe heard the phrase 'speed dating', she wanted to back away slowly and get out of the lunch bar as quickly as she could. "No. Absolutely not. I may be starting to get desperate when it comes to shaking up my life, but I'm not speed dating desperate just yet."

Heidi let out an audible whine. "Come on, Chloe! I know that this would be perfect for you! You remember me telling you that half of the cafe is on earth's side, and the other half is in Purgatory, right? It allows for the perfect mix-and-mingle of mortals and... well, us! You can be yourself around everyone there. Heck, you could probably even show up in your wolf form and everybody would cheer you. I know that you'll be able to find someone there who will *truly* accept you. Whereas, I think if I set you up with someone from my contacts, you might still feel like you have to hide. And I don't want you to have to do that with everyone anymore. Did you tell that friend of yours, Mackenzie, that you're a half-and-half yet?"

Chloe sighed and rubbed her temples, her elbows on the table. "Don't call me that. You make me sound like a pitcher of cream. I see what you're saying about finding someone who will really understand me, that's great, but I'm not doing the speed dating thing. The idea of that is so cheesy that not even an episode of 'Lucy' would touch on it."

Heidi turned around and looked at the television screen behind her. When she turned back around, she had a disappointed look on her face.

"I think that is *exactly* the kind of thing that this show would do because it's a *wonderful* idea! Come on, Chloe! Just go for one night, stay for the speed dating rounds, and if you don't end up finding anyone that you click with, I'll set you up with someone who I'm sure you'll like, okay?" Heidi asked.

LUCIFER

"Why don't you just set me up with that person right now?" Chloe asked, taking her final bite of her Dizzy Desi. "Why do I have to go to this cafe and suffer through speed dating in order to earn a date with them?"

Heidi shook her head and shoved the last bit of her sushi burrito in her mouth. Chloe could tell from the grimace on her face that she had discovered she should have eaten it all right when it was served to her, but she had to let her friend live and learn.

"I don't mean that I have them lined up for you right now," Heidi explained, picking a bit of seaweed from between her front teeth. "I mean, if you do try speed dating and it fails, I'll work extra hard to find you someone better. Deal?"

Chloe hesitated. She had a strong gut feeling inside telling her she shouldn't try out this speed dating. But then again, she had nothing else better to do. And besides, if the cafe was as accepting as Heidi said it was, shouldn't she give it a shot anyhow?

"Fine," Chloe said begrudgingly, and Heidi clapped excitedly. "But for every one of the dates I go on because of this stupid speed dating, you have to be ready on the other end of the phone in case I need an emergency rescue."

"Deal!" Heidi squealed excitedly. "Oh, Chloe, I'm so excited for you! I just know you're going to find someone as right for you as Dave is for me, and I can't wait for you to feel what that feels like. Here, let me call Aphrodite!" Heidi practically

LUCIFER

hauled her huge, pregnant belly over to the side in order to reach her phone.

"Aph...rodite?" Chloe asked warily, eyeing her friend and hoping she didn't fall off her chair. "As in—"

"The Goddess of Love, succubus, and former seductress, yes," Heidi answered hastily. "She and Eve, yes, *that* Eve of Adam and Eve, but they're divorced now so it's just Eve, run the Wednesday night speed dating!"

"The first woman of earth ended up divorcing her husband, the first man on earth, and now she runs a speed dating night?" Chloe asked skeptically.

"Yes!" Heidi said enthusiastically. "She's great, you'll love her."

Chloe's eyes opened in surprise and she was about to ask Heidi more about what she was saying, but she began dialing Aphrodite. She put the phone on speaker so that both she and Chloe could hear.

After a few rings, it clicked through.

"Hello?" a seductive voice answered.

"Hi, Aphrodite, it's Heidi!" the young pregnant woman said cheerily. "I have a favor to ask you."

There was a sigh on the other end of the line. "Yes, Heidi, what is it this time? Do you need another sexy demon to be your husband or something?"

Heidi laughed. "No, no, this time the favor is for my friend. She's in dire need of a good match, and I think coming to your speed dating night could maybe help her find her fated mate. She's the best girl you'll ever meet, and she just

LUCIFER

needs a little help."

There was a pause on the other end of the line, and then Aphrodite said, "I suppose I could work some of my magic with her. Tell her to come down to DeLux this Wednesday. I'll find her, don't worry."

The line went dead, and Heidi looked utterly thrilled. She began excitedly chattering about the speed dating night, and Chloe nodded along with her best friend, doing her best to feign excitement. The women chatted a bit more about men and dating, and then they settled up their bills, hugged, and parted ways.

As Chloe walked back to her car, she could feel the dread setting in.

What did I just agree to?

Why did I think I should ask Heidi for help?

I should have known she'd suggest something like this!

Shit.

I guess all I can do now is hope the speed dating part will be over as quickly and painlessly as possible.

Ugh.

Me and my big mouth.

CHAPTER FIVE

THE JOURNEY FROM Purgatory to earth was not a long one, but because Lucifer wanted to stay down in his kingdom, it felt like it took an eternity. He knew he could have just teleported there, or taken one of the many portals he had fashioned around Purgatory, but he felt like getting the exercise today.

LUCIFER

As he flew upward higher and higher, he could feel his appearance beginning to change; he was becoming human. He knew that his wings would remain until he was at the surface, but it always made him a little bit sad to see his demon features retract the higher he went.

When he could finally see the underside of the ground, Lucifer flew faster. He popped through the earth and his wings collapsed inside of him with such speed that no one around him on earth even noticed. He had shown up right outside of his apartment building, just as he'd planned.

He walked up the outdoor steps to his apartment and fished his keys out of his pants pocket. When he stepped in the door, he caught a whiff of himself and cringed.

Ugh.

Gross.

I'll never get used to the sulfur smell I get on me when I come back from Purgatory. I reek like a body that's been rotting underground for a month.

Which, Lucifer supposed, he had technically been doing, save for the rotting part. He quickly toed off his shoes and charged into the bathroom, disrobing and turning the water on to the correct temperature with lightning speed. He was just about to get into the shower when he caught a glimpse of himself in the mirror.

He decided he looked even better than usual, and flashed his image a cocky grin. He ran his fingers through his short black hair as he admired his features. When he hadn't been in his human form for a short while, he often forgot what he looked like.

Right, right. A jaw so chiseled it looks like it was sculpted from ice, prominent brow bone, well-maintained thick eyebrows, eyes so brown they practically look black, blemish free skin, full lips with a brilliant, white smile, sculpted body...

Damn.

No wonder all of the women throw themselves at me.

Lucifer slapped himself on the chest twice to pump himself up, and then he hopped in the shower. As the water sluiced down over his tight chest and ripped, six-pack abs, he couldn't help but think of all of the mischief he had gotten up to in this shower.

There was that time with Monica, the vampire... she liked to leave her marks.

Oh my, and the time with Lydia, the werewolf... She had a certain style she enjoyed. That was fun. He'd do her again, despite the howling. Yup!

And then the night with Ophelia, the siren... For some reason, I've never been able to get that woman out of my head.

Hmmm.

As he thought of the women from his past, his cock rose and demanded his attention. Stroking himself, he decided he needed to try and find someone at the cafe tonight. Self-satisfaction simply wasn't his preferred thing, and why

LUCIFER

should he when there were so many delectable options available out there to sample?

Oh hey, it's Wednesday. One of those speed dating nights that Aphrodite and Eve organize every month. Won't be too hard to find someone to fool around with.

Lucifer finished his shower, glanced once more at his delicious-as-sin body in the full-length mirror as he passed, and then dressed quickly, thinking of all of the potential partners he could meet up with tonight. He was feeling very aroused already, and so he decided it was better to get to the cafe in the hope that time would pass more quickly. He was a pleasure-driven man, and he didn't like having to wait to get what he wanted.

He was going to find someone tonight

and make them his.

Yes.

He liked the sound of that.

CHAPTER SIX

THE EVENING OF the seventeenth crept up on Chloe much too fast, and before she knew it, she was being ushered out of the front doors at work by a well-meaning Detective Diaz.

"Go on," Diaz said to her, pushing her forward with both hands on her shoulders. "I won't rest until I see you in your car driving away toward your speed dating night. If I don't see you walking out there right now, I'm going to quite literally kick your butt."

Chloe couldn't help but giggle as her friend and co-worker shoved her toward the door. "All right, all right, you can stop pushing and shoving right now. I can walk myself directly to my car from here. I won't even stop at the vending machine for a Mars bar."

Diaz stuck out her tongue like she was disgusted. "Blech. I can't believe that a full-grown, intelligent woman such as yourself is still eating candy bars. Especially Mars bars. Do you know how many chemicals are in there? I don't even want to think about it, to tell you the truth."

"Don't start with me on all of that 'clean eating' stuff you've gotten into," Chloe warned her. "I'm already so wary about tonight that if I have to think about watching what I eat while I'm there, I might not go at all."

Diaz' eyes widened, and she turned Chloe back around in the direction of the door and gave her a jokingly gentle kick on the butt. "Go! Get thee gone! No excuses, you're going to that mingle thing tonight and you're going to *enjoy it*!"

Both women laughed as Chloe walked out the door. She turned around one more time to wave at Diaz, and then she got into her Prius and drove home.

When she arrived, her clingy black cat, Atticus, greeted her at the door. He

LUCIFER always came right up to the front door and scratched madly at it the moment he heard her keys in the lock. Then, when she opened the door, he would get so excited to see her that he would just flop down, belly up on the floor. It was a terribly cute routine, except for the fact that Atticus had a tendency to do his tuck and flop right in the way of the door so Chloe had to shove the door against him in order to get into her apartment.

"Atty," she hissed at him, "move! I have a schedule to keep tonight, little buddy. I need in!"

Chloe was eventually able to coax Atticus out of the way of the door and gain entry to her small but comfortable apartment. That was one difference between Chloe and the strangulation victim from the other night: Chloe had some design sense and knew how to make her space a pleasant place to be.

She dropped her keys in the gold dish that her WolfMoon character's 3D model kept watch over and gave Remi a pat on the head. "Sorry, electronic friend. No playing for you tonight. I've got a date to keep."

Chloe must have been imagining things because she could have sworn that Remi's mouth turned downward into a frown at the mention of that. Shaking her head, she walked out of her front hallway, which she had worked very hard to wallpaper with a happy-looking light teal and yellow pattern. She thought it made the entrance to her space look like a French cafe, and that

LUCIFER

brought her a serious amount of joy.

To her left sat the living room, the biggest space in the apartment. It was a perfect square, painted the same teal as the wallpaper in her front hall, graced by a beautifully romantic fireplace on the far wall. It was electronic, of course, but that didn't matter to Chloe; she just liked the ambiance that it gave the room. There were WolfMoon trinkets across the top of the fireplace, and in the center, a wood-framed picture of Chloe's family. In the photo, a teenage Chloe stood in between her two younger sisters, Crea and Cara. Her mother, Neema, stood to the right of Crea, and her father, Tristan, had his arm around his wife. She was very close with her family, and called all of them at least once a week. Her parents were back home in New Jersey, whereas Crea had moved to San Diego with her husband, and Cara now lived in Fresno while she completed an internship at a news station.

Her favorite place to sit while she gamed, a butter-soft, white leather couch sat across from the fireplace. It was always covered in an assortment of colorful throw pillows and cozy blankets. Her desk, the same type of wood as the fireplace mantle, sat tucked in the corner but facing the big picture window along that wall. To the right of that was the kitchen. Chloe knew she got lucky enough to have a sliding door in the kitchen that led to a lovely balcony that overlooked the busy street below. Most of the units here faced other buildings

LUCIFER

with a boring view of brickwork and windows into other apartments across the laneway.

Chloe tossed off her boring work shoes and walked through the living room into her bedroom. It was the second biggest room in her apartment, and by far her favorite. She stored all of her best WolfMoon memorabilia on several shelves that spanned the walls in the room. Of course, she owned a bed that was so comfortable it was almost *too* comfortable. She always joked with Heidi that if she ever went missing, they should look for her in her bed; it had probably swallowed her up.

She walked over to her closet and opened it, unsure of what sort of outfit she was looking for. She wanted something that made her feel confident and cool, but not uncomfortable. A big fan of comfortable clothes, sometimes to a fault, she'd garnered the name 'Frumpy Frost' for a little while at work until Mackenzie had taken her shopping and remedied that. She didn't want to revert to the frumpy phase she'd worked so hard to overcome.

Chloe pulled out three potential outfits. The first was a pair of black leggings with a red strapless tank top that laced up in the back. As she stood in front of the mirror, though, she decided against it.

I feel too revealed.

Her next outfit, a navy blue dress that came down to just above her knee, had a v-neck with cute capped sleeves.

LUCIFER

The moment she put it on, she felt like a child. She didn't even bother looking in the mirror; she just tossed it off and went on to the third outfit.

The last outfit Chloe felt the most hopeful about. A sleek black dress, it fit her perfectly, hugged her curves, and accentuated all of the parts of her body that she loved the most. It was a comfortable length and didn't ride up when she walked, which was a huge bonus. It had straps crisscrossing her back, but not unsightly, too low ones.

Yes, the perfect combination.

Standing in front of the mirror, Chloe felt strong, confident, and happy with the outfit she had chosen. It brought out the iridescence of her hair, which ordinarily she would have avoided drawing attention to. However, tonight she was going to be around people who understood who and what she was, so it did not matter.

She checked the time on her phone: 7:31.

Oh no.

The speed dating started at eight pm sharp, and she hadn't even eaten anything yet. She flew around her apartment putting on makeup, running a brush through her hair, and shoving some leftovers in her mouth. Atticus followed her everywhere she went until she finally remembered that she had to feed him before she went. After she'd madly thrown his kibble into his dish and was ready to go, she checked the time again: 7:46.

LUCIFER

That was good enough. She slipped her feet into low black heels, then locked her door. She booked it down the stairs to her car. She slammed the car into gear, reversed out of her parking spot, and then raced across town.

She paid an exorbitant amount for parking, and despite the heels, then ran to the DeLux Cafe. When she came up on the door, she tried to dart inside but a bouncer stopped her.

"ID please?" he asked, holding his arm out to block her from going in.

"Are you—" Chloe started to protest, flashing him an incredulous look, but then sighed and backed down. She didn't have time for that. She whipped her ID out of her purse, handed it to the bouncer, and waited while he perused it at an agonizingly slow pace.

The bouncer laughed as he handed it back to her. "You're a lot older than you look. Sups downstairs, normals upstairs. Your choice."

Chloe rolled her eyes. "Yeah, thanks," she said sarcastically. The bouncer stepped to the side and let her in to the cafe.

As soon as she was actually inside, Chloe breathed a sigh of relief. It was now 7:58, which meant she had time to grab a drink before the speed dating started, hopefully. She descended the stairs and flipped through the red velvet curtains into an open space, and noted with a sinking feeling that she had to sign up for the event. There was a table off to the left with a red table cloth

LUCIFER

covered in red heart cut-outs with two pink boxes, one labeled 'Women' and one labeled 'Men'. There was a sign in front of the table that boasted 'Sign Up For Speed Dating Here!'. A cheery young woman with long, curly blonde locks, cobalt blue eyes, and the pointiest eyeteeth Chloe had ever seen sat behind the table eyeing her.

"Hi there!" the young woman called to Chloe. "Are you interested in signing up for our speed dating night?"

Chloe nodded, suddenly shy. "Yes, I am."

The girl looked as though Chloe had just told her she'd won a million dollars. "Really? Oh wonderful! Come on over here and I'll get you all set up, I'm Eve!"

Chloe slowly walked up to her and

could feel herself getting more nervous with every step she took. "Hi, Eve, I'm Chloe. Are... are you—"

"A vampire, yes!" she said gleefully, but then a horrified look came over her face. "Oh my god. Wait. Do you not know what type of a cafe this is? Are you a mortal?"

Chloe laughed and shook her head. She focused very hard on her right arm, and a second later, snowy white wolf fur started sprouting out of her skin. She stopped it before it reached its full length, however. Eve watched with fascination.

"I'm a white wolf shifter," Chloe explained, and then retracted her fur beneath her skin.

"Whoa," Eve marveled, grinning at

LUCIFER

her. "No matter how many times I see people transform, I'm never not impressed by it. Here's a ballot, just write your name at the bottom, grab a number from the next box, and then I'll take care of the rest!"

Chloe thanked Eve and then deposited her ballot in the box, snagged a red backed number card, and looked around for the drink counter. She saw it running the length of the back of the cafe, so she immediately headed in that direction. When she came up to it, there was a guy rummaging through some syrup bottles with his back turned to her. She assumed he was the barista, so she tried to get his attention.

"Excuse me?" she called, but the guy didn't turn around. "Sorry to bother you, but could I get a drink?"

The man didn't move, and for a second, Chloe thought he was outright ignoring her. But then, she saw a wire dangling from his ear and knew he was just listening to something. The problem was, though, now she didn't have any way of getting his attention.

That was when she noticed the mirror on the back of the counter. She started waving her hands, hoping he would look up. When he didn't, she just started waving them harder. Finally, she waved them as hard as she could and felt like a right idiot, which was of course the precise moment he decided to look up.

Of course.

Ugh.

I'm sure I looked like a total idiot!

LUCIFER

Their eyes met in the mirror, and Chloe felt as though she had been hit by lightning. A shocking sensation ran through her whole body, and for a moment, she worried that something terrible had happened. But as she looked deeper into the man's eyes, she realized the only thing that had occurred was that she had seen him. It was the most phenomenal feeling she'd ever experienced.

Chloe could have been imagining it, but she could have sworn she saw the man's eyes flare crimson around the edges momentarily. Perhaps this was a part of who this man was as a supernatural being. It was not unusual for supes to experience changes in eye color because of their non-human side.

GINA KINCADE & ERZABET BISHOP

Eventually, the two tore their eyes from each other and the man turned around to face her. He was quite handsome. He had short black hair and a jaw line so chiseled it looked as though he could cut glass with it. He was so tall, probably around six foot two or six foot three, that she nearly got a crick in her neck as she looked up at him. He reached to grab another syrup bottle to put it back in place and she observed he looked quite muscular, probably worked out at the gym daily, and had strong-looking hands. His nose twitched and she noticed it was quite pronounced, as was his brow bone, but it worked for his facial structure. He looked otherworldly, which Chloe also thought was not unusual at all for this cafe. However,

LUCIFER

unlike some of the other characters she had seen as she glanced around the room, this man seemed to have an air of darkness surrounding him. She wasn't sure if she liked that.

"What can I get you?" the guy finally asked, still holding his ear buds just away from his ears. She couldn't hear what he was listening to over the din of the room, but she was very curious to know.

"Uhmm..." Chloe said, feeling stupid that she hadn't thought of her order before she called him over. "What do you recommend?"

A smirk came across the guy's face. He threw both ear buds around his neck and let them dangle down his chest.

"What do I recommend?" he repeated,

amused. "Does that mean you want me to recommend something based on what I've concluded about you just from looking at you, or do you want me to tell you what I'm best at making?"

Chloe had been expecting the latter, but once he had mentioned the former, she became very intrigued by it. She summoned her courage and responded.

"Your recommendation," she said, her voice shaking only slightly.

The guy chuckled but said nothing, and then nodded in a self-satisfied way. He went to work grabbing bottles from beneath the counter that Chloe couldn't see, and then began measuring out different volumes of each liquid. She found herself almost hypnotized by the way he was creating her drink, but also

LUCIFER

wanted to have a bit of a surprise when he was done. She tore her gaze away for a moment to see what was happening in the rest of the room. She was very relieved to see it did not seem as though anything had started happening yet, even though it was now 8:03.

Chloe looked back at the barista, who was now shaking whatever he had mixed for her. Their eyes did not meet again, but she could almost feel his presence surrounding her. It was as though her soul reached out to him, and she couldn't figure out why.

Finally, the barista stopped shaking the drink and turned around to pour it. He made a few more movements, and then turned around and presented Chloe with her drink.

It was served in a tall glass, and was primarily an amber color. There were, however, small crystal like gems floating throughout the drink and the rim had been coated in an orange sugar. Sticking out of the top was a toothpick with a maraschino cherry poked on the end. Chloe nodded her head in approval, and then brought the drink closer to her to take a sniff and see what she could identify in it.

Chloe immediately recognized the smell. "An iced tea?" she asked the guy.

He nodded nonchalantly. "But not just any iced tea. My own secret recipe. You look like you're made up of a whole bunch of parts that if they weren't assembled in you as they are, they wouldn't be complimentary. But because you've worked on yourself a lot as a person, all your different parts are singing in perfect harmony... almost. That's why I chose an iced tea. It's a classic drink, but it could use a little more... spice."

"Spice?" Chloe repeated, slightly off put.

"Yeah," the guy replied. "That's why I put the cayenne around the rim, it kicks the iced tea up a notch. The crystals are because you're quite obviously a white wolf shifter. And the toothpick with the maraschino at the top represents me blessing you with my fiery presence."

Chloe just stared at the guy for a few seconds. This was not what she had been expecting at all. She had wanted him to make her some pretty, girly drink, pay her a few compliments, and then she'd go off and enjoy her speed dating. But instead, this guy had gone deep, and had drawn up some assumptions about her that she felt quite defensive about, especially because he had been able to tell them right away.

And the fact that he'd added 'himself' into the drink in such a cocky way turned her off even more. This guy obviously thought the world of himself, and Chloe decided right there and then, no matter what she had felt when she first looked at him, she was done with talking to him.

"Thanks," she said flatly, taking the drink and slapping some cash on the counter. "Keep the change."

She had wanted to leave him a tiny

LUCIFER

tip after a performance like that one, but she wasn't a monster. She tipped him the full twenty percent she tipped every other barista she'd ever had. As she carried her drink away from the counter and went to go find a seat, she couldn't help but grimace at the sight of the cayenne pepper on the rim. She had initially thought it was a nice sugar, but now that she knew what it was, she was absolutely dreading drinking it. She even went as far as to consider dumping it out in the bathroom.

"Alright friends and enemies, demons and other entities, lovers and... and... well, everyone!" a voice said over the sound system. "Who's ready for some speed dating?"

Chloe's focus was drawn away from

her drink as she turned around to see a woman with dark wavy hair in a skin-tight, bright red dress standing at the mic. She surveyed the room as if she owned it, which Chloe thought she very well may have. When the woman's deep sea blue eyes landed on Chloe, there was a flicker of recognition and she winked at her. It took her a moment to realize who the woman was, but then Chloe understood.

That must be Aphrodite.

Wow, she's even more beautiful than I imagined!

The crowd cheered in response to Aphrodite's announcement and she lapped it up like a kitten drinking milk. "Thank you, thank you. Could I please have all of the ladies take a seat on the right side of our line of tables here. You should have picked up a numbered card when you entered that will correspond with the table number you should sit at. Quick as you can, please."

Chloe nodded as if Aphrodite were speaking only to her, confirmed her table number as five, and moved gingerly through the crowd to take up her spot at the identically numbered table. She chose a seat beside a young woman with hair so red it looked like it might catch fire at any moment and another woman who looked unfortunately quite upset. She put her drink down on the table and hung her bag on the chair behind her, and then clasped her hands together, ready for the event to begin. After her interaction with the cocky barista, she no longer felt as nervous as she had when she arrived. She didn't have any desire to go home now; all she wanted to do was meet some people who were more fun than that barista.

"As always, the women have obeyed my instructions perfectly," Aphrodite said into the microphone, twirling the wire in and out of her fingers. She then walked off of the stage she had been standing on and came toward the crowd of men. There were so many of them that looked upon Aphrodite as though she were God's gift to earth. Chloe swore she even saw one of them drool. But as the seductress sauntered past each of the men, she paid them little to no attention. She seemed to be drinking in their auras and not caring about any looks they were giving her.

"Well, then," she said into the microphone, sounding pleased. "It seems that we have quite an assortment of gentlemen here this evening, both human and supernatural. Let's see if we can hook any of these fellows up with the right woman. Gentleman, please begin your travels at the table with the corresponding number on your blue cards, please."

Aphrodite then began walking around the room, watching and nodding as each man subsequently took a seat at a table.

As the men began getting divvied up, Chloe's heart began pounding a little faster. It was very exciting to have a man chosen for her, and even more exciting was the fact that she would be able to talk to them alone for a few minutes. She wondered who she would be getting paired with.

Ordinarily, Chloe might have been looking from man to man, trying to choose which one she thought was right for her. But tonight, Chloe decided that she was going to let fate and Aphrodite do that work for her and see how that went.

After what felt like an eternity of waiting, Aphrodite clapped her hands. A solo male remained, looking lost. He stood fairly tall with straight blond hair, brown eyes, and looked like he would fit right in with all of the surfers who gathered down around the Santa Monica pier. He was quite good looking, but not the type that Chloe would have

LUCIFER

ordinarily chosen. However, when Aphrodite pointed him in Chloe's direction with a nod, she wasn't about to cast her host's decision off to the side. When the man's eyes met Chloe's, they smiled gently at each other, and then he came to sit down in front of her.

"Hi," he said quietly as he took a seat.

"Hey," Chloe responded in a whisper. "I'm Chloe."

"Jackson," he said, extending his hand to her. She took it and shook it, and the two shyly looked at each other once again before they both looked off in other directions.

Okay.

Maybe this will end up going better than you thought.

You never know what might happen

when you get to talking.
   Let's see where this goes.

CHAPTER SEVEN

"ON YOUR MARK, get set... DATE!" Aphrodite cried a moment later after she'd explained the rules. She hit a button and a *bing!* sounded throughout the room. Chloe looked across at Jackson and smiled at him.

"So—"

"So—" They both started at the same

time and then stopped. When they realized what had happened, Jackson chuckled and then Chloe followed suit.

"You first," she said gently.

"No, no, I insist," Jackson said, waving his hands in front of him as a sign that he wasn't going to continue. "You probably had something far more interesting to begin with anyway."

Chloe ran her fingers through her silky hair. "Well, I'm sure both of our opening arguments were interesting. I was just going to ask you to tell me a bit about yourself." She flashed him a smile.

Jackson looked delighted. "That's what I was going to ask you too! Okay, then, I'll go first, I guess. I'm Jackson Downs from Laguna Beach and I'm a surfing instructor. If you ask me, I think it's the best job in the world for a million reasons, but the main one being that I get to shift into my alternate form as soon as my job is done for the day."

"Oh wow, you're a shifter, too?" she asked, engaged. "What is your alternate form?"

Jackson smiled shyly. "A great white shark."

Chloe's eyes widened. "You? A great white shark? Wow, that's so interesting!"

"What about you?" Jackson played with the moisture on the outside of his glass as he looked into Chloe's eyes.

"Guess," she said teasingly, crossing her arms in front of her and smiling at him.

"Oh god, I'm terrible at guessing," Jackson said, fluffing his hair as he spoke. "But I'll give it a shot."

He then proceeded to look her up and down while rubbing his chin thoughtfully. After a few moments, he looked back up at her.

"Are you... a palomino horse?" he guessed.

Chloe shook her head. "Oooo, no, sorry, but great guess! I'm a white wolf."

Jackson looked at her in surprise. "Really? That's incredible! I've never met a white wolf shifter."

Right then, unfortunately, Aphrodite came over the microphone once more. "Thirty seconds, people!"

Jackson and Chloe looked at each other, mildly panicked.

"This went so much faster than I thought it would," Chloe said, shaking her head.

"I know, right? I guess they call it 'speed dating' for a reason," Jackson joked. He and Chloe then looked at each other, both unsure of what to say.

"So..." Chloe said, finally breaking the ice. "Should we... I mean, do you want to exchange numbers?"

"Yes!" Jackson said enthusiastically, but then seemed to worry that he'd been too excited. He cleared his throat. "I mean, that would be nice, if you'd like to."

Chloe nodded, surprising herself. "Yes, that's great. Here, I'll give you my number and then you can text me."

She then recited her phone number off to him and Jackson immediately texted her. She smiled down at her

LUCIFER

phone when it arrived, and then looked back up at him. She heard the *bing* of the timer go off again and Aphrodite came back on the microphone.

"All right everyone, time to switch it up!" she shouted.

"Well, it was nice meeting you," Jackson said pleasantly to Chloe.

"You too," she responded, and then just like that he was on to the next woman. She had to admit that she didn't mind this form of dating because it took out so much of the awkwardness that was created because of expectations. She enjoyed her brief moment with Jackson and would certainly be texting him later, but she was also looking forward to whoever she was going to meet next.

GINA KINCADE & ERZABET BISHOP

Over the next hour, Chloe met so many men that she could hardly keep track of them. There were certainly a few duds who she wrote off immediately, but there were also quite a few possible gems. She had gotten the numbers of a vampire named Ethan, a werewolf named Flynn, and an Irish Pooka named Rory. She hadn't even known what a Pooka was until Rory explained it to her.

"Essentially, I'm a trickster spirit," he'd said with his eyes alight. "I like causing mayhem that is just good fun and doesn't do anyone much harm. For instance, at night, sometimes I like to enter people's houses and rearrange a few things so that they think they've sleep walked in the night. I always enjoy that one a lot, because I get to have a good chuckle at it, but they do, too."

Chloe had liked the sound of being amused by little pranks here and there, as long as no one got hurt and everyone found them funny, and so she'd gladly given him her number when he asked for it. Those four were the ones that had stood out the most to her throughout the night, and she was very pleased with that.

When the speed dating wrapped up, Chloe was very much ready to go home. She pulled out her phone to see what time it was, and when she read '10:10', she was mildly ashamed at how tired she was. When she had been younger, she used to be able to stay out until all hours of the night. Now, however, all she wanted was to be at home in bed, curled up with a good book.

She collected up her bag and slipped her phone back in her pocket, and then her gaze landed on her drink. It still sat on the table in front of her, completely full. She recalled the barista who had handed her the drink, and when she thought about him, she knew she wanted to leave it right there on the table, untouched.

I'm not going to play your stupid game, you jerk.

Enjoy dumping this down the drain later.

But just as Chloe turned around to make her way to the door, she practically ran right into Aphrodite.

"Whoa, there," said the beautiful seductress, putting her hands out in front of her to stop Chloe. "What's your hurry, human furry?"

"Sorry!" Chloe said, catching herself before she actually hit her. "I was so focused on my... Well, it doesn't matter. I wasn't watching where I was going. My apologies."

"No worries," Aphrodite responded casually. Then, she peeked around behind Chloe and looked at the full drink on the table. "You weren't thirsty?"

"Ahhh..." Chloe said uncomfortably. "No, not really."

"Really? If there was something wrong with your drink, we'd be happy to make you a new one, free of charge of course," Aphrodite offered.

"Oh no, no, that's okay, really," Chloe backtracked quickly. "I ordered something I didn't really feel like having after all, but thank you so much for offering."

Aphrodite shrugged. "Suit yourself. So, did you enjoy the speed dating tonight?"

Chloe nodded enthusiastically. "Very much so! I met four really nice guys who I'm very excited about meeting up with."

Aphrodite raised an eyebrow. "Oh really? Who were they?"

Chloe then recounted the four men, and after each one, Aphrodite looked increasingly disappointed and Chloe couldn't figure out why.

"All right, then," Aphrodite said curtly, obviously giving Chloe a fake smile. "Well, I'm glad you found some potentials here tonight, that's what I like to see. Do you know what you're looking for in a mate?"

Chloe was a bit taken off guard by the question. "Looking for? As in... what exactly?"

"Like what boxes does your guy have to check," Aphrodite clarified. "Tall, short, athletic, likes to take things a bit easier, vampire, werewolf... What's your type?"

Chloe cocked her head to the side, slightly dumbfounded. "Oh. I... I don't think I've ever really considered that before. I just sort of try and go into everything with an open mind, and then if I feel a connection, I pursue it."

"Mmmm," Aphrodite purred, seeming to have enjoyed her response. "That gives me a better idea. Connection. And did you feel an instant connection with anyone here tonight? Anyone at all?"

Chloe thought back through the four guys whose numbers she had gotten and realized that she hadn't exactly felt a spark with any of them. She was about to tell Aphrodite that she hadn't felt a true connection with anyone... until she thought of the feeling she'd had when she laid eyes on the barista.

Yes, but then look what sort of a guy he turned out to be.

How could I feel a connection with anyone that shallow?

Chloe shook her head. "No true connection with anyone, I'm afraid. But that doesn't mean it won't develop over time as I get to know them."

Aphrodite chuckled, putting her hand

on the back of the chair and leaning on it. "Ahh, Chloe. I'm sure you could make a deeper connection with one of them if you wanted to, but if you didn't feel something... novel when you looked at any of them, then I don't think you're meant to be. What we strive for here at the DeLux cafe are the meetings of fated mates and true loves. When you meet that person... well, I've never experienced it myself, but I've heard it described as being struck by lightning. You feel a rush through you unlike anything else. And you're absolutely sure you didn't feel that with anyone tonight?"

Chloe opened her mouth to respond right away but then hesitated.

Did... did she say lightning?

No.

No, that can't be true.

There is no way what I felt when I looked at that barista was me looking at my fated mate.

Not that guy.

Nope!

"Sadly, no one," Chloe said simply.

Aphrodite narrowed her eyes as if she didn't believe her, but then said, "Chloe, do you believe in fated mates? Is finding yours even something that we should be striving for?"

"I... I think I do," Chloe said nervously. "I mean, Heidi found her fated mate in Dave here at the cafe, so who says I won't find mine here, too?"

Now, Aphrodite looked very pleased. "Wonderful. I'll do a little bit of digging and see what I can find for you."

Aphrodite winked at her and walked away, sashaying as she went. As Chloe watched her walk away, she could have sworn she felt the barista's fiery red eyes upon her, but when she looked around she could not see him. Shrugging the feeling off, Chloe turned around to grab her bag, and then took one last glance at the drink on her table.

I've heard it described as being struck by lightning.

As Aphrodite's words rang in her head, Chloe lifted the glass to her lips and gingerly took a sip. She was completely blown away; it was by far the best drink Chloe had ever tried in her life. The flavors blended together so nicely, and she was pleasantly surprised by the way the red powder on the rim complimented the drink. She chuckled to herself and shook her head.

I can't believe it.

That guy was right!

Chloe looked around the almost empty cafe one last time, trying to locate the barista. He was nowhere to be found, and so Chloe finally decided it was time to go home. She'd had enough excitement for one night, and now it was time to see which of the men she'd met tonight would pan out.

CHAPTER EIGHT

AS LUCIFER STOOD by the exit of the Underworld cafe with the white-haired woman walking straight toward him, he felt like he wanted to pounce on her. He was using his powers of invisibility, of course, so she couldn't see him, but he really hoped she could still sense him. The moment he had seen her when he

LUCIFER

turned around behind the counter, he knew he had to have her. His beast, deep inside of him, screamed out to him, demanding to be heard and taken seriously.

You have to meet her.

You have to meet her and you have to be with her.

She is our fated mate.

Mine!

Lucifer had been so stunned by the sensation he felt when he looked at her at first, his mind hadn't even worked properly. He registered that she was saying things to him, but he couldn't figure out how to respond. He did say something in response, of course, otherwise he would have looked like a total creep.

He began fixing her a drink on autopilot, but as he was doing so, he realized that this was his first chance to impress her. He stopped what he was doing and began thinking over all that he had been able to sense about her. At first, little came to mind, but then his demon senses went into overdrive and started telling him too many things about her at once. He tried his best to sift through them so that he could make a drink that would knock her socks off. When he finally finished, he decided to add the cayenne pepper on the rim at the last minute.

When he presented it to her, he was incredibly proud of himself. She, however, looked utterly unimpressed, and possibly even annoyed. She'd said

LUCIFER

very little to him after that point, simply giving him a tip and taking her drink. When she walked away, it felt like a little part of him died. He couldn't believe he had so royally ruined their first encounter.

She was getting closer to him now, and she smelled so amazing that he could hardly control himself. Her scent, a mix of sweet cherries and cool morning air, drove him wild. He wanted to whisper something into her ear and brush his lips against her neck so he could breathe her in even deeper. But as she came right up to him, all Lucifer could do was reach out to her.

As she passed him, his fingers grazed the back of her neck. The woman froze and he could see a shiver dance up her spine. It brought him great delight to know his touch had tantalized her.

He wanted more.

She, however looked around one last time and then quickly went out the door. The moment she was out of his sight, he regretted his decision.

You fool!

You should have spoken to her, stopped her from leaving, or done anything to make her stay with you!

How could you lose her like that?

Mate!

Lucifer took off his invisibility and saw Aphrodite walking across the room to the drink counter. He rushed over to her and commanded her attention.

"Who was that?" he demanded, taking her wrist and pulling her closer to him. Aphrodite smelled like fresh roses and petrichor—a very pleasant combination, but not one Lucifer found utterly enthralling in the way he did when Chloe's scent filled his nose. "You were speaking to her there at the end, who was she?"

Aphrodite laughed in a self-satisfied way. "Oooh, looks like someone has a crush. Her name is Chloe. Chloe Frost. She's a friend of a friend who came here tonight looking for her next relationship. But it looks like you might like her in a bigger way than just a crush... You. Lucifer Morningstar. Confirmed lifetime playboy. Can it be you've finally met your match? May I say you look smitten, darling!" Aphrodite smirked at him and winked.

"Yes. Well, no, not smitten. I'd never be— Ugh!" Lucifer was so aroused he could hardly contain himself and his thoughts spun all over the place. He knew they shouldn't be talking about this out in the open, and he couldn't admit to her that Chloe was his fated mate, or at least his beast thought so. Flustered, he grasped her by the arm, dragged her into his nearby office, and closed the door behind them.

"Sit," he ordered, pointing at the client chair in front of his desk. He sat down in his luxurious chair at his desk, and Aphrodite did as she was told. They stared at each other, hard, both waiting for the other to begin. Finally, Lucifer caved.

"I need you to tell me everything you

know about her so I can find her again. I'm not going to let her get away."

"Get away?" Aphrodite teased him, crossing her arms in front of her and raising an eyebrow at him. "Good goddess, use other language. You sound like you're going to kill the poor girl."

Lucifer rolled his eyes. "You know what I mean. Go. Tell me."

But Aphrodite did not look like she was going to spill her guts about who this Chloe woman was. "I'll tell you just enough to leave you feeling satisfied. She's a special detective with the homicide department of the LAPD. She's also a white wolf shifter, as if you couldn't already tell that from her radiant hair. And she's single, thankfully."

Lucifer nodded along with all of the information Aphrodite imparted. "Good, good. More."

Aphrodite shook her head. "Absolutely not. You're going to have to discover the rest for yourself."

Lucifer was suddenly incensed. "By myself? How do you expect me to find her again if all I know is where she works, what her paranormal abilities are, and her relationship status? You can't be serious!"

Aphrodite laughed out loud. "Lucifer, I've told you absolutely everything you need to know. You're the King of the Underworld, this should be a very easy task."

Lucifer flared his nostrils but did not allow his anger to get the better of him.

LUCIFER

He knew if he exploded in front of Aphrodite, it wouldn't do him any good. She had a power over him no one else did right then, and so he decided to heed her advice.

"Fine," he grumbled, leaning back in his chair. "I'll find her and make her mine, and then I won't thank you for helping us at all."

Aphrodite rolled her eyes and glanced out the window to his left. It was now dark outside, but the moon was shining so brightly that its light bled into the room.

"All right, all right," Aphrodite conceded, "I guess I can help you a little more. You know how much I like it when you're indebted to me. Why do you like her so much, anyway?"

Lucifer looked up at her quickly. She smirked at him once again, as if she knew exactly why he was asking about Chloe. But he didn't want to give Aphrodite that satisfaction, and so he decided to admit nothing to her.

"She's beautiful," he said curtly. "I have to have her."

Aphrodite nodded, not believing a word he was saying. "Fine. I'll accept that answer for now, but I must say I'm surprised by this kind of a reaction from you, Lucifer. You've bedded more women from this cafe than I care to count, so why is it just one woman caught your eye tonight? And what stopped you from going right to her and claiming her for yourself? Are you changing your ways?"

Lucifer shook his head sharply, in full

denial. "No. Absolutely not."

"Then describe to me any other girl that you saw in the cafe tonight," Aphrodite said with a taunting look on her face. "Absolutely anyone. I need to make sure you didn't have your eyes just on Chloe all night."

Lucifer panicked for a moment, unable to think of anyone else he'd seen. He tried to run through his memory, desperate to prove Aphrodite wrong. Finally, he thought of the young woman who'd sat next to Chloe.

"Miserable looking, black greasy hair, almost pure white eyes, black dress, blue high heels," he told Aphrodite. "Do I win a prize now?"

Aphrodite looked unimpressed. "Absolutely not. That just tells me you're not completely consumed by this girl, which I'm happy to hear. This also means I'm going to be nice to you and set up a date for you with Chloe next Wednesday night."

Lucifer felt the heat as his eyes flashed red, and did his best to return them to their normal color as quickly as possible. "Excellent. I will be expecting her at seven pm, in my—"

"No," Aphrodite stopped him. "You're going to go wherever I tell you and meet her for as long as I say. If you wanted my help with this, you should have known that it would be on my terms, okay?"

Lucifer growled at her and Aphrodite laughed. Standing, she put both of her hands on the table and leaned in toward him until their faces were mere inches

LUCIFER

apart.

"Don't you know that doesn't work on me anymore, Lucifer?" Aphrodite purred. "Ever since I discovered I can feed off of other people's relationships, I haven't needed you anymore. Does that hurt your feelings?"

Lucifer laughed in her face. "You go have your fun getting your kicks off of watching other people be happy. I'm going to find myself a temporary new partner and feel the arousal first hand."

Lucifer got up from his desk and opened the door, holding it for Aphrodite. She turned around and adjusted her dress, never making eye contact with him. As she passed him, she whispered, "I do hope you enjoy your date with Chloe next week. You never know where it could lead you..."

And then, Aphrodite sashayed out of his office and back into the cafe. As he watched her go, his thoughts were only on Chloe. He pictured her radiant white hair, her perfect heart-shaped face, and her sumptuous, curvy-in-all-the-right-spots body. He wanted to fly out into the night and find her right now so he could claim her as his own. But he knew if he were patient, and waited until next Wednesday night, the payoff would be so much better. He gently closed the door to his office, sat down in his chair, and let his thoughts wander to naughty fantasies about Chloe.

He would have her, soon.

He would make her his.

Mine! Mate! His beast agreed.

LUCIFER

CHAPTER NINE

TWO NIGHTS LATER, Chloe was all set to have her first real date with one of the men she'd met at the DeLux cafe speed date night. Jackson. She had to admit this was the date she was the most excited for, and when he'd suggested they take a walk along the beach to a nice beachfront restaurant, she had

LUCIFER

jumped at the opportunity. It had been so long since she'd been to Laguna Beach, but she remembered loving it and longing to return to it.

As she got dressed for the date tonight, she put on a shorter, tighter-fitting dress than the one she'd worn the night of the speed dating. It was a pretty cobalt blue color, made her eyes pop, and she actually felt very sexy, which was not something she felt too often. She chose a pair of comfortable sandals that she knew would be easy to walk in the sand with and then, without bothering to check herself in the mirror a second time, she headed out the door.

The drive to the beach took a little longer than she thought it would, but that was fine because Chloe always left extra time. When she arrived in the beach parking lot, she was happy to see that Jackson wasn't there yet. That gave her a few minutes to touch up her makeup and make sure that she felt ready for the date.

Everything is going to go fine.

He seems like a really nice guy, and I'm sure the two of you will hit it off.

If nothing else, it's a beautiful night for a walk on the beach!

Chloe smiled at herself in the mirror. For a split second, she could have sworn she saw the glowing red eyes of the barista from the DeLux cafe staring at her from the backseat. She gasped, turned around, and of course the backseat remained empty. Giving her head a shake, she chuckled to herself.

LUCIFER

You're losing it, Chloe.

Don't even try and get me to think about that guy.

If anything is meant to happen with him, it will happen naturally.

For now, focus on Jackson and the date tonight.

Right then, Chloe looked out of the driver's side window and saw Jackson pull up in his car. Her heart started beating a little bit faster and she felt her palms begin to sweat, but she didn't let herself get carried away. She sucked in a deep breath, centered herself, and then got out of the car.

As soon as they saw each other, they both waved. Jackson took another minute to collect his things from the car, and then he got out and locked it. They walked toward each other, and when they got close, Chloe wasn't sure how to greet him.

Do I hug him?
Do I just say hello?
What do I do?

Thankfully, Jackson seemed a little less nervous tonight than he had at the speed dating. "Hi, Chloe!" he said warmly, waving at her again. "Thank you so much for agreeing to this beach walk."

Chloe laughed. "Thank you so much for suggesting it! I think we picked the perfect night for a beach stroll, we couldn't have asked for better weather."

They both looked out over the water and smiled. "You're absolutely right," Jackson agreed. It isn't too windy, there are hardly any clouds, and that should make for a perfect sunset. Shall we go?"

Chloe nodded, and the two set off toward the sand. They then walked down right to the water, and Jackson looked back at her.

"Is it going to weird you out if I take off my shoes while we walk?" he asked her.

Chloe shook her head adamantly. "Absolutely not! I was just thinking I might do the same thing."

They both took a moment to take off their shoes, and then they dipped their toes in the water. They walked along, their feet gently treading in the shallow water, and neither of them said anything. Chloe drank in the beauty of the surroundings and all of the magnificent sounds that came along with them. The waves lapped so peacefully upon the shore, the seagulls cried overhead, and in the distance, Chloe could hear some jazz music wafting out of the speakers at the cafe they were headed toward. It couldn't have been a more perfect location.

"So," Jackson finally began, sounding hesitant. "Have you always lived in Los Angeles, or did you grow up somewhere else?"

"I actually grew up in New Jersey," Chloe informed him, swishing the water with her foot as she walked. "I moved out to LA when I got my job with the LAPD. I've been in love with the city ever since."

"New Jersey, that's cool," he said

LUCIFER

genuinely.

Chloe chuckled. "It's actually not, really. New Jersey is one of the least exciting states in the whole country, if you ask me. I would take LA over NJ any day. What about you, did you grow up here?"

Jackson nodded. "In California, yes, but not LA. I'm from Santa Barbara, actually, but I moved here because the pay for instructors was a little bit better at the tourist hotspots."

"Ahhh, of course," Chloe answered, smoothing her hands over the top of her dress. She was still very happy with the clothing choice she'd made, but she was beginning to notice that the dress was ruffling every few steps. After fixing it a few times, she decided to just let it be.

"So all of the tourists who come to LA to learn how to surf never know that they're really being taught by a great white shark?"

Jackson laughed. "You're absolutely right. But if you ask me, I think anyone who isn't a paranormal like us should be put in a different part of the city. That way, they can keep their naiveté that we don't exist and we can shift whenever we'd like."

Chloe looked at him, surprised. "You... you think that we should be in different parts of the city?"

Jackson nodded emphatically. "Absolutely. It would make our lives so much easier. Can you imagine waking up and going into work with other people like you? Wouldn't cases get solved so much faster if you could just shift at will?"

Chloe's brow furrowed. In the distance, she imagined that there was someone standing on the beach and it *might* have looked like they were waving a red flag.

"Uhm... no, not really," Chloe said gingerly. She hadn't expected a problem between them to come up so early in the date. "If all of my co-workers had to be paranormal beings, there wouldn't be enough people to work in the station. We're pretty few and far between in the city, as far as I know. Plus, if we were closed off in a certain part of the city, wouldn't we be miserable? One of the things I love about LA are all of the places I can go to nearby."

"Oh, I'm not saying that *we* couldn't travel to other places," Jackson explained as if that suggestion was utterly preposterous. "The humans just couldn't come into our part of the city. We could put a force field up around it!"

Jackson seemed genuinely thrilled by the idea, but the more they talked about it, the more Chloe began to see exactly what Jackson was trying to say.

"So... we should get an area of Los Angeles dedicated to us where humans can't enter? Is that what you're saying?" Chloe asked hesitantly. She didn't really want to hear his answer to the question, because she figured she already knew what he was going to say. She had really hoped that out of all of the guys who she had set up dates with, Jackson was

LUCIFER

going to be the one who would come out on top. Right now, though, she realized she might have to end the date early if this was the way he thought.

"That's it, you've got it!" Jackson said encouragingly, and Chloe also noted a hint of condescension. "Because we're superior to humans, we should definitely have a designated area of Los Angeles all to ourselves. It'd be perfect!"

Chloe's heart sank. As she looked down the beach, she could now clearly see the person she had been imagining with the flag was now waving it madly above their head, and the flag was very, very red. This was a red flag that she couldn't ignore with Jackson, and she knew she needed to end their date before it went any further. She had no time for guys like him.

Chloe stopped walking and turned to face Jackson. It took him a second to see she'd stopped, but when he did, he came back and stood in front of her.

"Jackson," she said firmly, "I think your views are erroneous, hurtful, and downright awful. You shouldn't think for a second that just because we're paranormal we're superior to humans. I'm going to go back to my car now, and I don't want you to text me again. Do you understand?"

Jackson looked positively stunned. "What? How could you turn on me like that? You sounded like you were agreeing with me, and then you turn around and say this? What's wrong with you?"

LUCIFER

"Absolutely nothing. Goodbye, Jackson," Chloe said decidedly, walking away from him.

"Chloe, wait! You can't just leave me like this!" he shouted after her. "We're on a date, you owe me to see out the rest of the date!"

Chloe stopped and turned back to answer him. "I don't owe you anything, you slimeball, and the fact that you just said that makes me even more sure that I don't want to see you again. Go get some therapy, learn why your views are outdated and toxic, and then we'll talk. Maybe."

With that, Chloe marched back to the car and didn't listen to one more thing Jackson shouted after her. She drove home, absolutely furious she had wasted most of a perfectly good night on that prejudiced jerk.

When she got in the door to her apartment, she immediately changed out of her dress, tossing it into the dirty clothes basket, and put on her most comfortable outfit. She grabbed a glass of wine and logged into WolfMoon.

Yes.

A perfect switch from a horrible evening.

About an hour later, her stomach started growling, the hunger pangs distracting her from her gaming. She walked down to her favorite Korean restaurant a few doors down and ordered takeout. When she got home, she decided to put on a movie, and after she'd finished eating, she and Atticus fell

LUCIFER

asleep on the couch before the movie was even halfway done. It ended up being the nicest evening she'd had in a long time.

CHAPTER TEN

TWO NIGHTS LATER, she had a date set up with Ethan, the vampire. After her disastrous date with Jackson, she felt a little more hesitant about this one, but she was still certain it would go well. They were going bowling, so Chloe chose to wear something a little more casual. She ended up choosing a pair of high-waist, bleached jeans that perfectly hugged her curves and a flowy maroon top that made her feel a bit like a 70's model. She even went as far as to complete the look by trying to fan her hair the way that Farah Fawcett used to, but it didn't work very well.

She arrived at the bowling alley about fifteen minutes early, and surprisingly, Ethan was already there. When they saw each other, Ethan immediately opened his arms to hug her, and she gladly took the greeting; it saved her the trouble of having to make a decision about what to do.

When they pulled away from each other, Chloe took a moment to admire her date. He had dark hair and dark eyes, but his skin was as pale as a sheet of paper. But his paleness didn't detract from his good looks; in fact, it was quite the opposite. His paper white skin made him look ethereally gorgeous, and Chloe suddenly felt more excited to be going on this date with him.

"Thank you so much for agreeing to this kind of a silly fun date," Ethan said gratefully, shoving his hands into his pockets and looking a little embarrassed.

"This is the best kind of date, in my opinion," Chloe said, smiling at him. "I love bowling but I haven't done it in so long, so this is perfect."

"Excellent," Ethan said, chuckling. He held up his bowling shoes and said, "I've got my own pair of shoes, so how about we get you a pair?"

Chloe nodded enthusiastically.

LUCIFER

"You've got your own pair? As in, you brought them with you?"

"Yup," he confirmed for her. "They make you buy a pair as soon as you start playing professionally."

Chloe stared at him, shocked. "P-professionally? You're a professional bowler?"

Ethan nodded, looking a little perplexed. "I didn't tell you that? Huh. That's weird. Yeah, I bowl for a living. It's the perfect job for me. I hardly ever have to go out into the sun!"

Chloe laughed and then glanced around the alley. As she looked at the people bowling, she realized they were all either teams practicing or people on their own who were getting strike after strike. She then looked overhead and saw all of the ribbons and trophies of achievement hanging from the ceiling. Suddenly, she realized what this place was.

"Oh my gosh," she said quietly. "I thought we were just playing a casual game of bowling. But this... this is like where you go to practice for your games?"

"Oh god, no, don't worry. I wouldn't do that to you," Ethan said reassuringly. "No, we're just going to have a fun game! It doesn't matter who wins or loses. I just thought it would be a nice thing to do while we talk, and then maybe after we can get a drink or something?"

Chloe felt slightly less intimidated, but she still wasn't sure about this. Still, she gave him an encouraging nod and followed him to get her some shoes. They found a suitable pair quite quickly and were set up at lane five. Ethan looked pretty cute setting up their names in the computer as 'Wolfie' and 'Vamp', and after that, they were ready to get started.

"Would you like to go first?" Ethan asked her, gesturing to the lane and giving her a winning smile.

Chloe grimaced. "Oh, I don't know. I think maybe you should go first so I can see what you do and copy you."

Ethan chuckled and reached under the seat, pulling out a rounded suitcase. Chloe felt befuddled by it until she saw him unzip it and pull out a bowling ball.

"Sure, I'd be happy to go first," Ethan said, rubbing his ball with his hand. Chloe stared at the ball, somewhat mystified as to how it had gotten there.

"I take it that's your own ball?" Chloe asked him, gesturing to it.

"Yes, and this is the lane I always use," Ethan explained. "But again, I promise, we're only here to have a good time. I'm not going to try and like... use you as practice or anything."

They both laughed, and finally Chloe began to feel a little more comfortable. Ethan walked up to the line, readied himself, and then gently sent his ball down the lane. It went in a perfectly straight line and took down all of the pins in one fell swoop. Chloe applauded proudly.

"Beautiful!" she congratulated him, but when Ethan turned around, she could see that he was not pleased. "Is

LUCIFER

something wrong?"

Ethan let out a dramatic sigh, but then put on a brave smile. "No, no, I just... That was the worst shot I've made in a long time, and I'm trying not to beat myself up about it."

Chloe felt baffled. "But... but you got a strike?"

Ethan rolled his eyes. "Yes, but did you not see the curve in my ball? The strike was sheer dumb luck. I'm lucky I got anything on that one."

Ethan came and sat beside her, and Chloe could tell he was still feeling quite moody. She let him sit there for a minute, and she felt very uncomfortable because he wasn't saying anything. Eventually, he looked up at her, and she hoped he would say something that might save the direction that their date was going in.

"Well? Are you going to go next?" he growled.

Chloe raised her eyebrows at him, shocked he would talk to her in that way, but then decided not to say anything for the time being. She got up, picked up one of the balls to the right of the lane and walked up to the line. She readied herself, aimed for the center of the lane, and then shot her ball down toward the pins. When she saw that it knocked down every last one of them, she jumped and cheered, looking back to Ethan to see his excitement, too.

Ethan was staring at the pins, looking furious.

"Are you kidding me?" he said,

standing up and walking toward her. "You got a perfect strike on your first bowl?"

Now, Chloe was getting angry. "Yeah, isn't that great?"

Ethan shook his head. "No! You shouldn't be better at this than I am! Give me that."

He snatched his ball off of the tray and Chloe stepped back, absolutely fuming. He stepped up to the line, aimed his ball, and then let it go. This time, it traveled much faster and far less straight. It went straight into the gutter without even so much as touching a pin.

Ethan didn't say anything, nor did he turn around to look at Chloe. She had to put her hand over her mouth to stop herself from laughing too hard. He grabbed another ball, readied himself, and then tried again. It went straight into the gutter as well.

Chloe's eyes widened and she held her breath, waiting to see what would happen to the third ball. She could tell Ethan was getting angrier because he was balling his fists as he stood at the top of the lane.

He stomped over and grabbed another ball, not even bothering to stop and aim before he chucked it down toward the pins. The ball danced all over the lane until it finally landed… right in the gutter again.

For a moment, Ethan did nothing. He stood at the top of the lane, frozen in disappointment. Chloe wasn't sure if she should say anything or stand up and try

LUCIFER

to talk to him. To be honest, she didn't want to do either. It was clear this guy had some pretty major anger issues as well as obvious problems with self-confidence.

If he doesn't react well to this, I'm just going to get up and leave.

Chloe waited for just another minute and then Ethan finally started moving. He turned around very slowly and faced Chloe, but did not make eye contact with her. He then walked right over to where he'd put his things on the bench, undid his bowling shoes, and put on his outdoor shoes. He tied the laces of his bowling shoes, slung them around his neck, and then walked back to the lane to pick up his personal bowling ball. When he put it in his bag, Chloe knew exactly what he was going to do next, which was exactly what he ended up doing. Without saying a word, Ethan walked away from their bowling lane, opened the door to the outside, and left.

For a few minutes, Chloe was so stunned by what had just come to pass that she couldn't begin to wrap her head around it. The whole situation was so bizarre! She had never met someone as childish as Ethan, and she couldn't believe a grown man would really just get up and leave his date because the bowling game that he'd chosen wasn't going his way. Chloe felt utterly baffled.

But then suddenly, she began laughing.

At first it was a quiet, reserved laugh that barely made any sound, but then it began to get louder. She couldn't help herself.

He threw a tantrum!

He threw an honest-to-goodness tantrum because he couldn't bowl as well as he usually could.

I can't believe it.

I just can't believe it.

By now, Chloe was laughing so hard and so loud that everyone else in the building stared at her. She didn't care, though. When she finally managed to regain her composure, she stood up, walked to the top of the lane and grabbed a ball. When she shot it down toward the pins, it knocked everything over in one go and she clapped for herself. She then proceeded to finish the rest of the bowling game all by herself.

When she looked around toward the end, there were still a few people staring at her, but she didn't mind.

I paid for this game, and I'm having a great time, so I am going to finish this!

I don't care if I look crazy bowling by myself after having laughed hysterically.

That Ethan was... something else, and I'm having a great time now.

Why would I want to stop just because people are staring at me?

Once more, Chloe made the most of her evening. Why let another crappy date ruin her fun. Who needed people like that anyway!

CHAPTER ELEVEN

BY THE TIME Chloe got to her third and final date, she no longer felt the least bit nervous. Her first two dates had been so disastrous that at this point, all she could hope is she came away from tonight with a funny story to tell Mackenzie on Monday morning. She was seeing the Pookah named Rory tonight,

LUCIFER

and that excited her a little. She'd never met or heard of a Pookah before she'd been introduced to him, and she was curious to see what he'd be like. Judging by the mischievous nature he described the night they'd met at speed dating, she had a feeling they were going to get up to something fun.

Chloe met him at sunset just in front of the Santa Monica pier. It was just dark enough that the ferris wheel at the end of the pier had its lights on, and the restaurant on this side of the pier was filled to the brim with hungry people.

As Chloe walked up to the pier, she noticed a couple holding hands as they walked toward her. The woman of the couple held a large stuffed bear that they'd obviously won at one of the cheesy booths on the pier, and the man looked toward her very proudly. Chloe guessed this probably meant the young woman had won the bear for herself and her date was thoroughly impressed by her, but she didn't want to assume. A part of her wanted to stop and ask them what had happened on their date, but that would have been... creepy. Instead, she focused on scanning the crowd for Rory with his bright red hair and freckled cheeks.

She didn't see him initially, which wasn't a problem. She checked her phone and realized she was still a few minutes early. She decided to walk to the side of the pier so she could look out over the beach and watch the sun dip below the watery horizon.

LUCIFER

The sunset tonight looked simply breathtaking, and as Chloe walked to the side of the pier, she thought that even if tonight's date didn't go well, she was at least happy to be here to witness this sunset.

Resting her arms on top of the railing, Chloe leaned over and looked out toward the water. The orange, red, and yellow colors of the sky ricocheted off of the clouds and painted them cotton candy pink. The water also reflected the radiant colors of the sunset, and as Chloe watched, a surfer danced across the top of the waves toward the horizon.

She then looked back toward the beach and marveled at the sheer width of the beach. It had to be at least half a mile wide, if not wider. That was one of the first things that had really stuck in Chloe's mind when she'd moved here, and it never stopped impressing her. Even a beach like Venice was a monstrosity to be reckoned with, in her mind.

Chloe continued staring at the sunset until the sun fully disappeared below the water. It started getting darker almost by the second, and Chloe wondered how they were going to be able to enjoy their walk down the pier and onto the beach in pitch blackness. She turned around and checked for Rory once again, but still did not see him.

Perhaps he's gone onto the pier and is waiting for me there.

I'll take a little stroll that way and see if I can find him.

LUCIFER

Chloe turned to her right and started walking down the pier. There were a great many people there to watch the sunset who had all gathered around the railings to look, leaving the center mostly free for her to walk through. Chloe kept her eyes peeled for Rory, but saw no familiar faces in the crowd. By the time she reached the other end, it was getting quite dark, and she was starting to get worried.

She pulled out her phone and pulled up the conversation she had been having with Rory.

Hey! I think we got our signals crossed. I haven't been able to find you yet. Where are you?

She pressed send, and then tapped her phone against her hand as she waited for a response. Rory had been so quick on replies thus far that she figured it wouldn't be too long before he replied.

She was right. A moment later his text came through.

I've been looking for you too! I'm standing right by the door to the restaurant on the pier. I'll wait here?

Sounds great! Be there in a sec.

Chloe slipped her phone back in her pocket and high-tailed it back to the front of the restaurant. She felt renewed excitement as she walked up to it, but when she got there, there was no familiar looking red-haired guy standing by the door. Chloe circled around the whole restaurant three times, convinced she must have been picturing the wrong door. However, when she came up to the

LUCIFER

front after the third time and he still wasn't there, she pulled out her phone once again. She could feel her wolf wanting to burst forth as she became more frustrated, but she took a few deep breaths to try and keep that desire at bay for the time being.

I'm standing right by the door. I don't see you, am I missing something?

After hitting send, Chloe kept looking around. It was now after dusk and the mosquitoes were starting to come out, which annoyed Chloe even more. She had to keep moving around to stop from getting eaten alive.

Her phone buzzed and she looked down at the message, her annoyance barely remaining below the surface.

Sorry! I thought I saw you, so I went to

chase after you, but I realized it was someone else. I'm heading back toward the restaurant now. Stay there!

That seemed like a fairly reasonable mistake, and so the frustration ebbed away a bit. She stood right beside the door, where he said he had been standing, pacing back and forth so that the mosquitoes wouldn't get her.

She waited there for another five minutes before she'd had enough. She picked up the phone and called Rory. He picked up within two rings.

"Where are you?" she barked, a bit of her wolf coming out. "I've been waiting here for so long!"

And then, to Chloe's infuriation, she heard Rory burst out laughing on the other end of the line.

LUCIFER

"I was just playing a bit of a prank on you!" Rory said through his laughter. "You know, my Pookah side coming out a little. Stay where you are and I'll be there in five minutes."

"No!" Chloe shouted at him through the phone. She had now reached the point of no return with her shifting, and was going to transform into her wolf form within the next two minutes. "That was cruel and unnecessary. I'm not going to go on the rest of this date with you, goodbye."

Chloe hung up the phone before Rory could even say anything else. She then had to start running as fast as she could; she needed to get somewhere where no one would see her shift. The closest place that she could think of was under the pier, and so she ran there. By now, the beach was mostly vacant because it was so dark, and Chloe was incredibly grateful for that. She raced down underneath the pier in amongst the wood that was holding it up and began to transform.

It felt so good to shift into her wolf form this time. It was kind of like finally being able to reach that itch you could never quite find on your back. As her fur popped out and her nose elongated into her snout, Chloe felt a bit of her anger at Rory disappearing. She had fully transformed within a minute, and when she had, she stood there looking out at the water. She wanted to run through the wilderness, but there wasn't exactly anywhere she could go from here.

LUCIFER

Sighing, Chloe jumped up onto the first wooden pillar, and then onto the next one and the next one. It felt kind of like she was a ball pinging around a pinball machine because the pillars were all at different angles. Chloe had never tried parkour, but she could imagine this was probably what it felt like.

Soon, she bounded from pillar to pillar over the water, and the spray from the ocean felt so wonderful in her fur. By the time that she got to the end of the area beneath the pier, she found a small platform she discovered she could perch on. She sat down on it, the breeze off the water cooling her after her athletic sprint. She panted, her tongue hanging slightly out, and could immediately taste the saltiness of the water.

Her thoughts turned to Rory, the idiot who'd had so much fun taunting her for his own pleasure, and while it had made her feel incredibly angry at first, it now just made her laugh.

I can't believe he thought I was going to stay for the date after he did that. What kind of fool does he think I am?

And to do this to a white wolf shifter?

Does he not know that I could tear him a new one with my teeth?

Chloe chuckled to herself, but of course because she was in her wolf form, it came out as a kind of growl. Suddenly, she could have sworn she heard someone else laughing with her. She whirled around, looking to and fro.

What she saw, however, was nothing more than the waves and the wooden

LUCIFER

pillars leading back to the beach. Even with her heightened vision, Chloe couldn't see anyone or anything there with her beneath the pier. She looked around for another second and then decided she must have just heard the water make a strange noise.

Chloe still couldn't shake the feeling there was someone or something down there with her. She stood there with her paws on the wet wood for a long time, trying to focus and see who it was, but in the end she found no one.

I must be losing my mind.

CHAPTER TWELVE

AS HE LEVITATED in front of Chloe in her white wolf form there beneath the pier while being invisible, Lucifer couldn't explain what was happening to him. The more he stared at her, the more he was dying to be with her. The urges he felt toward her weren't normal for him. Quite the opposite, actually. For

LUCIFER

the first time in his eternal life, Lucifer dreamed of just holding this woman and spending time with her instead of his usual carnal desires. And that was very unsettling to him.

He didn't dare get any closer to Chloe, because he feared she might be able to sense him with her heightened abilities. He felt fairly certain she could tell someone was there now regardless; he just didn't want her to know it was him.

Lucifer had secretly followed Chloe on all of her dates while he was invisible. He couldn't bear the thought of her meeting with success on any of them, so he watched with a tiny bit of unabashed glee as each one failed.

Chloe was gradually starting to come down from her rage-induced transformation, and so Lucifer knew that he didn't have much longer to stand there and admire her. He drank every moment in. He loved the way her glistening white fur blew in the wind and little droplets of water from the ocean collected on her elegant snout. Lucifer had never been attracted to anyone like this before, this obsessed, so this was a very new sensation for him. At one point, Chloe seemed to look right into Lucifer's eyes, and he knew that he had to leave right then, otherwise he might be spotted.

Lucifer dove straight into the water. He thought about the surprise that Chloe would have seeing the ripples on the surface but without evidence of anything having jumped into the water and he chuckled.

What else could he have done?

His ability to become invisible was one of Lucifer's favorite powers as the ruler of the Underworld. As he swam down further and further into the water, he felt himself turning back into his demon form. His wings popped out of his back but remained in a streamlined position so as to not hinder his ability to glide through the water. He could feel his nails lengthening, sharpening and becoming tougher, and by the time he burst through the bottom of the ocean, he was fully back in his demon form.

It took him another few minutes of downward travel to return to Purgatory, but when he arrived, the heat of the flames upon his face woke him right up.

Ahhh.

It's so good to be home.

As Lucifer flew toward his palace, he took some time to see how the new demons were doing now. Flying over them, he noted they were completing their demon training with ease, and a few of them were even beginning to develop into their final demon forms.

Flying into his bedroom through the window, he landed on the ground with a *thud.* Immediately, he heard heavy paws coming down the hall, and a minute later Fenriz thundered through the door and came to a sudden halt in front of Lucifer. The enormous hellhound sat down in front of Lucifer as he had been taught to do and growled in pleasure at the sight of his master.

LUCIFER

Lucifer brushed his fingers through his hair, dislodging some of the water that had gotten in his hair during his trip through the ocean, and then petted Fenriz.

"How's my loyal hound? Did you get into any scrapes while I was away?" Lucifer asked him.

The dog barked two very deep, guttural barks at his master, which meant *yes.*

"Good boy," Lucifer applauded him, presenting him with his favorite treat: freeze-dried black widow spiders. The hellhound gobbled them up and then jumped into his bed right at the foot of Lucifer's.

Lucifer shook the rest of the water off of his wings, his clothes already dry from the heat in the underworld on his trip down, and then he lay down in bed, musing over the last few days.

He felt very pleased by all of the decisions he had made in regard to Chloe. He was going to make her his, and everything he had done so far had been to ensure that. Now, however, he still had to wait until Wednesday to finally have the chance to talk to her.

Lucifer groaned audibly and rolled over onto his stomach. He was not used to being made to wait; it was something that made him very frustrated. All he wanted to do was kiss her and hold her in his arms for a long, long time. He wondered what her lips would feel like against his. He needed to taste her and feel her curves under his hands before

LUCIFER

he took her to heights she'd never imagined. His cock ached, and he knew he couldn't focus on thoughts of Chloe lying naked beneath him for too long, otherwise he would be driven to distraction. He had to get out of bed and do something, otherwise he was going to go mad with desire.

Lucifer climbed out of bed and began pacing the room. He tried to think of something, anything, to make the time go faster so that he could be with Chloe.

Maybe I could go and raise some hell somewhere out in Purgatory...

No, I don't even feel like doing that.

I could create some new laws that my demons would have to obey and watch them suffer...

Ugh.

No.

I don't much feel like doing that either.

What I do feel like doing, however, is placing my lips on the side of Chloe's neck, hearing her sharp intake of breath, waiting a beat to make her suffer in anticipation... and then plunging my teeth into her and making her my own.

Damn it.

Double damn it.

I have got to stop this!

These thoughts are not helping.

Lucifer growled. His manhood throbbed, his balls pulled up tight, and he could feel his eyes turning fiery red with his desire. He felt like a virgin thinking about his first sexual experience, for devil's sake.

What the hell?

LUCIFER

I'm better than this.

I control everything around me and yet I can't even control my desire for a woman now?

He slammed his fist against the wall next to the window, his breaths coming fast and furious now, his chest tight, heart pounding with anticipation.

"Enough!" he roared aloud, startling Fenriz. The hellhound growled and flashed his master a look as if to say "what the hell" and Lucifer realized he needed to regain his control.

He finally decided to just go for a fly somewhere, cause some mayhem in his kingdom. That was about as much as he could concentrate on for now, anyway. He would just have to find simple pleasures to distract him until he could be with Chloe.

CHAPTER THIRTEEN

THE DAY AFTER Rory stood up Chloe, she texted Heidi to tell her what had happened. But before Chloe could even get into the specifics of her first disastrous date with Jackson, Heidi begged her to meet her in person.

"I can't stay in the house any longer," Heidi said in her text. "Dave keeps trying to make me stay inside because he's so worried about the babies, but I need out! Let's go back to Bejewels and you can tell me everything."

Chloe agreed to it, and that evening, the two women met up at the restaurant.

As Heidi slid into the chair with a grunt and a groan, Chloe noted that her friend somehow looked even more pregnant now, which concerned her. Heidi wasn't supposed to be getting this big so soon, but somehow she had become literally enormous.

All Chloe could do was hope the supernatural doctors were doing their job and keeping an eye on her friend. She knew Heidi kept complaining about Dave hovering over her and her frustration with it, but she could commiserate with the demon-dad-to-be now that she'd seen Heidi's size. Hopefully the delivery went as smoothly as possible. She couldn't bear the thought of her bestie having any complications.

"No way," Heidi said, her jaw hanging open when Chloe finished telling her about her third and last date. "He just stood you up like that? I thought Pookahs were only supposed to engage in fun, harmless pranks, not ones that make you waste an evening of your life."

"I thought so, too," Chloe said sadly, poking at her food with her fork. "I so hoped that in one of those guys I might have found someone to at least fool around with for a little while. Maybe my standards are too high, maybe it's my fault and not theirs." She gulped, imagining her future filled with the same lame type of men.

"Hold the phone," Heidi said, stopping her negative musing. "This is the furthest thing from your fault! You just somehow got paired up with three of the dudiest duds in all of dudsville!"

"Right, but who picked them out of the lineup of guys at the speed dating night?" Chloe asked her best friend. "I could have chosen so many other men, but instead fate and those blasted number cards chose those three for me. Doesn't that say more about me than it does about them?"

Heidi shook her head emphatically. "It absolutely does not. There are so many men who come off as charming and cool when you first meet them and then they show you their true selves once you're out on a date with them. That's exactly what happened to you. I was lucky with Dave and it was the other way around. He came across as a bit of a nerd when I first met him, but then I got to see how cool and charming he really was. Yes, fate had a hand in it, sure, but I know it had to be *him*. We were simply made for one another," Heidi gushed and then sighed, a blush staining her cheeks

Chloe chuckled and took a swig of her drink. "You're one of the luckiest women in LA, Heidi."

"Don't I know it!" Heidi said gleefully, but then she suddenly grabbed her stomach and a pained look crossed her

LUCIFER

face.

"Heidi?" Chloe asked, reaching across the table to grasp the hand that wasn't on Heidi's stomach. "What happened, do you need me to take you to the hospital?"

"No," Heidi said, still wincing in pain. "It's not that bad. Dave took me to the doctor's yesterday because the twins were doing this then, too, and apparently it's Braxton-Hicks contractions."

Chloe's eyes widened and she felt the color drain from her face. "Contractions? Doesn't that mean the babies are coming? We have to get to the hospital!"

Heidi laughed a little through her pain but shook her head. "No, no, these are just the rehearsal contractions.

They're getting me ready for the real thing and might I say, I am *not* looking forward to the real thing. These ones are bad enough."

Chloe chuckled, very relieved that she didn't have to take her to the hospital, and kept holding her friend's hand until the Braxton-Hicks contractions subsided.

Finally, Heidi let out the breath she had been holding and smiled at Chloe. "There we go, all better," she said, as though the intense pain had been nothing at all, really. "Now, I'm about to ask you something that sounds kinda stupid, but I promise I'm one hundred percent serious."

Chloe furrowed her eyebrows. "Is this a question I'm going to like?"

LUCIFER

"It isn't a question, it's a request," Heidi clarified, putting a forkful of dinner into her mouth. "And... I think you're going to hate me for it." She shrugged.

Chloe rolled her eyes. "I hate you for most of your suggestions, so go right ahead."

Heidi laughed. "That sounds about right. Okay then, here goes: You need to go back to the DeLux Cafe for one last kick at the speed dating can."

Chloe laughed out loud and picked up her sushi burrito to take a bite. When she had finished chewing, she replied flatly, "Absolutely not."

"What did I say?" Heidi responded, wiggling her finger at her. "I'm serious. I know you had a horrible time of it with the men this time around, but I have a very, very strong feeling that if you go back to DeLux for one more night of speed dating, you won't be disappointed."

"Heidi, I would love to make you happy and do as you ask," Chloe began, "but I didn't really want to do this speed dating thing in the first place. I can't waste more of my time going back to the cafe and doing that speed dating all over again. That just isn't going to work."

Heidi reached out and took her hand, looking sincerely into her best friend's eyes. "I completely understand, and I don't ever want to force you into anything you don't want to do. But this time around, I'm just asking you to trust me for a little longer. I know your first experience there ended up being utterly rotten, but I can almost promise that if you go back for the speed dating again, you won't be disappointed."

There was something about Heidi's tone that told Chloe she knew something that Chloe didn't. Chloe narrowed her eyes.

"Heidi..." she said warningly, "what do you know that I don't?"

Heidi faked a surprised look and Chloe could have guffawed at the sight of it. "Me? Nothing. Absolutely nothing. I just have a very strong feeling about this next speed dating, Chloe. Will you believe me for just a little bit longer and go one more time?"

Chloe sighed, closed her eyes, and when she opened them, she was standing outside the front doors of the

GINA KINCADE & ERZABET BISHOP

DeLux Cafe. Or at least, that's how quickly it felt the time flew by between Chloe agreeing to go back and her arrival at the cafe. Heidi had even convinced her to wear a sexier outfit this time—a tight jean miniskirt with a black strapless tank top. She felt so revealed wearing this outfit that all she wanted to do was hop back into the cab and go home. But she had made a promise to Heidi and she intended to keep it, so she sucked in a deep breath and opened the door.

Chloe went through basically the same motions as last time. She trudged down the spiral staircase, through the red curtains. She greeted Eve at the front table, grabbed her number card, and looked around the dark room at all the other singles who had gathered. And then, she walked to the counter to get herself a juice drink.

When she got there, however, the barista she'd had before wasn't working this time. Instead, she got a pretty brunette barista. Chloe couldn't believe she felt a little bit disappointed the other guy wasn't there. It wasn't that she had liked him or anything—that would have been bizarre. She just felt like trying a bit more of that iced tea than she'd had the last time. Or so she convinced herself.

After Chloe got her drink and turned around, she practically ran right into Aphrodite. The succubus wore another gorgeous red dress and looked as much like a temptress as ever.

"Sorry!" Chloe squealed, pulling back

her drink so as to not spill it on her.

But Aphrodite was unmoved. "Nothing to be sorry for, love. I was the one who crept up behind you. But I'm glad I caught you before you sat down. You're not going to be speed dating tonight, after all."

Chloe's brow furrowed. "I'm... I'm not?"

Aphrodite shook her head. "Nope. I've got a special date set up for you tonight."

CHAPTER FOURTEEN

AT LONG LAST, the night had arrived. Lucifer felt so pent-up he could have exploded into a fireball at just the thought of seeing Chloe. He spent way too long trying to figure out what outfit to wear tonight, but he finally landed on his usual black jeans, black dress shirt buttoned up to the top with the sleeves

LUCIFER

rolled up to his elbows, and a black leather belt. He wanted to make sure that when his eyes glowed red, she'd undeniably be able to see it.

When he arrived at the cafe after flying up from Purgatory, he first went to go and say hello to Eve. He had been so caught up with Chloe the last time that he hadn't even talked to Eve, an unforgivable sin to his old friend. Tonight, however, he made sure she was the first person he connected with.

"Lucifer!" Eve cried in a cheery voice from behind the registration desk when she saw him. "I'm so glad I got to see you tonight before your big date!"

Lucifer chuckled a low, sexy chuckle. "Is that what it's being referred to around here as?"

Eve grinned at him. "If it wasn't before, it sure is now! Aren't you excited? You finally found your fated mate!"

"To tell you the truth, Eve," Lucifer said, leaning in close to her, "I'm thrilled. Couldn't be happier."

Eve squealed a little and clapped her hands. "Yay! Well, go get ready. Aphrodite will send her your way when she arrives!"

Lucifer thanked her, and then intended to head straight to the private table where he and Chloe were going to meet. However, when he realized just how many people were in the room for the speed dating night, he figured it would be a good idea to mingle with a few of them. If nothing else, it would keep people coming back to the cafe if

LUCIFER

they knew the owner himself attended the speed dating nights, too.

And so, for the next fifteen or so minutes while he was waiting for Chloe to arrive, Lucifer mingled with the guests, said hello to the new faces, and welcomed back the return patrons. It actually helped him quite a bit to talk with people so he wasn't so worked up while he waited for Chloe. There were quite a few people there who he knew, which made him happy. It was nice to be surrounded by friendly faces.

After a little while of this, however, Lucifer began to get anxious again. The speed dating start time crept closer and closer, and Chloe had still not shown up yet. Lucifer ran his fingers through his hair, glanced around the cafe once more to make sure that he hadn't missed her, and felt dejected to see that he had not. He was beginning to worry that she would not come at all.

To stop himself from spiraling down into worry any further, Lucifer went and got himself a drink. They'd hired a barista to replace Adam, and so far she was doing great. Lucifer didn't know what to order because he was so distracted, so he just went with a Shirley Temple. It was a sickly sweet drink, but the blood red color of it satisfied him immensely.

Right after he'd gotten his drink and took his first sip, however, time seemed to slow. Suddenly, everyone in the room moved in slow motion except for him, and as he turned to look at the velvet

LUCIFER

curtains that led into the speed dating section of the cafe, he saw them rustle.

And then, his heart stopped.

Chloe stepped through the curtains wearing an outfit so sexy, he didn't think he was going to be able to contain himself. His eyes widened and his breath caught in his throat, but he knew he had to get back to the corner table so that he could surprise her. He forced himself to slide silently out of the main part of the room before she could lay eyes on him and slid into the red booth at their table.

While Lucifer waited, he could think of nothing else but Chloe—the way her hair seemed to radiate light, the curvature of her hips, and the way her lips seemed to call to him. He couldn't believe he was finally going to talk with her tonight. It was better than anything he could have ever imagined.

After what seemed like an eternity, Aphrodite poked her head through the curtains sectioning off their booth. She smiled playfully at him and mouthed 'are you ready?'

Lucifer nodded emphatically, and then Aphrodite disappeared. Lucifer smoothed back his hair and tried to decide on what position he should be in when she first saw him.

Should he have his arm over the chair back?

Should he be sitting relaxed?

Should he be—

Before he had time to decide, the curtain was drawn back. Chloe stood

LUCIFER

there with one hand on the curtain, looking at him, an utterly perplexed look crossing her features. His heart stopped for the second time in ten minutes when their eyes met. He got the same electric lightning strike feeling he had the first time he'd laid eyes on her, so he knew that was good. Chloe, however, did not look as impressed.

"Sorry, I'm looking for a private... meeting," Chloe said, looking slightly uncomfortable. "I think I came into the wrong booth."

"I don't think you did," Lucifer said seductively, flashing his meg-watt smile at her.

Chloe continued to look befuddled. "But you're... you work here, don't you? You're the barista who made me that iced tea the first time I was here."

Lucifer nodded. "How did you enjoy it? I never got to ask."

Chloe opened her mouth to answer and then a strange look came across her face. Lucifer couldn't decipher it, and he didn't like that.

"To be honest I... I didn't really drink much of it," Chloe replied honestly. "You were so smug when you gave it to me that I didn't want to."

Lucifer looked at her, surprised. "I... I was too smug giving you your drink?"

Chloe nodded and crossed her arms in front of her chest. Lucifer knew he wasn't supposed to be looking but he couldn't help but notice that the new position accentuated her breasts even more. She looked incredible.

LUCIFER

"Yeah, it kind of made me uncomfortable," Chloe responded. "The drink tasted delicious, like nothing I'd ever had before, but I couldn't enjoy it because of how rude you had been."

Lucifer felt utterly delighted by this. He had never had a woman talk to him like this before. Everyone always fawned over and flattered him, which, although it was very nice, got a little bit tiring after a while. This... her forthright and honest attitude... felt so new and exciting. His cock hardened, pressing against the zipper of his jeans.

"I'm not going to apologize for being confident in my drink-making skills," Lucifer said, his voice coming out growly as he tried to hide the increased blood flow to down below, and then softening the growl with a wicked smile on his face. "But I will apologize for making you feel like that. Can I make it up to you?"

Chloe raised an eyebrow at him and uncrossed her arms. That was a good sign.

"I'd like to make you another drink," Lucifer said. "Would you be kind enough to give me a second shot?"

He watched Chloe ponder the offer for a moment, and then slowly nodded.

"Wonderful," he whispered, getting up from the booth. "Follow me."

CHAPTER FIFTEEN

CHLOE HESITANTLY FOLLOWED Lucifer to the drink counter and watched as he kindly asked the barista if they'd mind if he made her drink himself. The young woman nodded and lowered her gaze to the ground.

"I'll go on my break, then," she said, lifting her head and smiling back up at

LUCIFER

him. She turned on her heel and disappeared behind the curtain at the end of the counter.

As Chloe watched, Lucifer looked after her and then sucked in a deep breath. When he turned to look at Chloe, it was as if they'd never met before. He gave her a very charming smile and then approached the counter.

"Hi there," he said warmly. "What can I get for you?"

Chloe felt a little bit silly. She hadn't realized he was going to pretend not to know her. If he had told her that, she might have declined this offer. But they were already in it, so she decided to let him give it a try. The worst thing that could happen is she could end up with a boring drink.

"What do you recommend?" Chloe said, just as she had the first time they'd met.

The corner of Lucifer's mouth turned up a little higher.

"What do I recommend?" he repeated, just as he had before. "Does that mean you want me to recommend something based on what I've concluded about you from the look of you, or do you want me to tell you what I'm best at making?"

Chloe chuckled and leaned up against the counter, resting her chin in her hand. "Your recommendation."

This time around, however, Lucifer didn't look smug. Now, he looked ecstatic.

"It would be my pleasure. Could I first ask you what you'd like for your juice

LUCIFER

base?"

Chloe nodded and then looked past him at all of her choices in the bottles. "Hmmm... How about cranberry?"

Lucifer scoffed a little, making Chloe feel unimpressed, but he quickly explained himself.

"Sorry about that," he said genuinely, a brilliant smile crossing his features. "That was a bit of my personal preference coming through. I hate cranberry juice with a passion... But, for you, I think I can work with it."

He turned around and grabbed a tall glass off the sideboard. He filled it halfway with cranberry juice, and then he spun to face away from once more so Chloe couldn't see what he added to the drink. She heard bottles being taken off the shelf and then liquids being poured. At one point, he even grabbed one of the nozzles off the counter and squirted something from there into her glass. Finally, he grabbed a plastic sword, a lime wedge, and a toothpick with some paper fills on the end. He fiddled with the glass for a second, and then turned around and presented it to her.

The liquid in the glass before Chloe looked like a cheerful sunset. The cranberry juice looked to have been mixed with orange juice, grenadine, and likely a little bit of sprite, she thought. It was topped with the lime wedge that had been speared with the sword, and the toothpick with the paper firework on top stuck out from the top. It was a heavenly color, and Chloe immediately brought it

LUCIFER

to her lips for a sip. The moment it touched her tongue, Chloe felt the same sensation that she had the night she'd finally tried his iced tea. It not only tasted amazing, there was also something else underneath it. This time, Chloe could decipher what that undertone was—desire.

She looked up at Lucifer, who looked back at her, his dark eyes filled with anticipation. She kept her face neutral, put down the drink, and then responded to him.

"That... was disgusting." She scrunched up her face as best she could and shoved the drink back in his direction. "What made you think I would want to drink something like that?"

As she watched, Lucifer began to

squirm and she relished in it.

"Really? I thought you would love it. It's just the right combination of sweet and fruity," he said, scratching the back of his head anxiously. "I can make you something different, here."

Lucifer went to grab the drink but Chloe put her hand on it first. Their eyes met and she relinquished her joke about not liking it and smiled at him.

"I'm kidding," she explained, flashing a smile. She took the drink back and gulped down another swig of it to prove her point. "This is actually really good."

Lucifer looked momentarily annoyed, and then he seemed to change his mood. He chuckled and replied, "Thank the devil for that. You were about to make me think I'd lost my powers of

LUCIFER

perception."

Chloe giggled and continued drinking her concoction. The pair stared at each other for a moment, unsure of what to do.

"Well, what do you say?" Lucifer asked, gesturing toward the booth they'd left. "Do you think you might be able to tolerate me?"

Chloe shrugged with a small smirk on her face. "I suppose if you can make a drink as good as this one, you might be worth keeping around for a short time. Here," she said, taking some cash out of her wallet and offering it to him.

Lucifer laughed and moved out from behind the counter. "It's on the house. If you hadn't liked it, then maybe I'd have made you pay for it."

GINA KINCADE & ERZABET BISHOP

Chloe chuckled. She felt far more relaxed now as they walked back to their private booth. When they got behind the curtain, Lucifer sat on one side and Chloe slid into the other. It was a half moon booth, and so they weren't staring straight at each other. It did, however, succeed in making it feel much more intimate because it felt as though they were enclosed in a little space together.

"I realize I never introduced myself," Chloe said, putting her small purse down beside her and her drink on the table. "I'm Chloe Frost."

She extended her hand, expecting the man to take it and shake it. Instead, he took it, rotated it so that the back of her palm was facing up, and then lifted it to his mouth and brushed his lips across her hand a feathery light kiss. The move surprisingly smooth, Chloe rather liked it.

"Lovely to meet you, Chloe," he said seductively, his eyes glittering. "I'm Lucifer Morningstar."

She could have sworn she saw his eyes flash red around the rim for a moment just as they had the first time they'd met, but she brushed it off.

Lucifer...

Nah...he couldn't be...could he?

Chloe gave him a timid smile. "Nice to meet you, too, Lucifer."

They paused there with Lucifer holding Chloe's hand in mid-air, staring into each other's eyes. As they did, Chloe began to feel like he was trying to tell her something, but she couldn't figure out what. When they finally let go, Chloe took the hand that Lucifer had been holding and cradled it within her other one on her lap. It tingled in the best way possible.

"So Chloe," Lucifer said casually, leaning back in his seat and taking her in, "tell me a bit about yourself. Where are you from? What do you do for a living? Where do you live now?"

This was the normal stuff that Chloe had been expecting from her first three dates. This was all she had ever wanted—just a nice, casual date where they could talk about themselves, chat a bit about their mutual interests, maybe a kiss or two, and then call it a night. As they spoke more, Chloe began to have bigger hopes for tonight.

LUCIFER

"Well," Chloe began, "that's an awful lot to tell, but I'll do my best. I grew up with my parents and my sisters, I have two of them, in Macon, New Jersey. I started out there with the NJPD as an officer, and then gradually worked my way up to detective. When I got the job out here as a special agent, I knew it was time to move out. I came to LA, found an apartment in West Hollywood, and I've lived there ever since. I live alone in a one bedroom with my cat, Atticus, and when I'm not working... who am I kidding, I'm hardly ever not working."

Lucifer chuckled, and the sound of his laughter made Chloe's heart flutter.

Maybe my first instinct about this guy was wrong after all. He does seem to have changed his tune, and he is so incredibly good looking. But what could an attractive guy like this see in me? He's probably only going on this date with me out of pity because Aphrodite made him or something.

"All right," Lucifer replied. "That was a pretty good start. And what makes you an acceptable client of this cafe?"

Chloe raised an eyebrow at him. "Sorry, what?"

"I mean," Lucifer clarified, "what are you besides human? You have to be some sort of supernatural being if you're a part of the clientele here."

"Oh, I understand you now," Chloe responded, and then she caught his eye and gave him a playful smile. "Do you want to try and guess?"

Lucifer looked highly intrigued, but

LUCIFER

also a little aroused. It was a good combination of things.

"More than anything," he said. He looked her up and down, squinted his eyes at her and then put his hand over his mouth, his finger thoughtfully rubbing along his bottom lip. Suddenly, his eyes flashed between dark and crimson again for a split second. "Hmmm... a white wolf shifter?"

Chloe's eyes sprung open as surprise rushed through her. "How did you know? That can't have just been a good guess, how did you find out?"

Lucifer laughed. "I'd like to claim intuition, but I overheard you chatting during the last speed dating night."

Chloe joined in on the laughter, relieved. "Of course, right, how could I have not realized that? So, yes, I'm a white wolf shifter. I'm still a part of my home pack, the Macconwood pack. Our Alpha is Rafe Maccon."

Lucifer nodded along with her. "That's incredible. I've always thought white wolf shifters are some of the most gorgeous beings of all. I'm acquainted, however briefly, with your Alpha's reputation. Good man, that one. Won't see him around my home anytime soon, though, I'm sure."

Chloe looked at him, trying to discern if he was serious or not, and what he meant by the quip about her Alpha. He gazed back at her, eyes unblinking, and so she knew he had to be serious about his compliment at least. She felt her face flush and glanced away from him, her gaze dropping to her lap.

"T-thank you," Chloe stuttered, pushing some of her long white hair behind her ears. "No one has ever said anything like that to me before."

When Chloe heard silence in response to her comment, she looked up. Lucifer was staring at her, looking quite dumbfounded.

"How absurd! How is it even possible no one has ever complimented you on your glorious beauty before? That is something we need to quickly rectify," Lucifer said assertively, a growl rumbling up from his chest.

The way he looked at her, his gaze intently studying her face and then roving over her curves, made Chloe feel slightly aroused as a rush of heat filled her core. He had such an intense dark stare and it made his features look even more attractive.

"Chloe, you are the most beautiful woman I've ever met. The moment I saw you last time, I knew I had to have you. Are you aware of how truly stunning you are?"

Chloe scoffed and heat filled her cheeks as butterflies tumbled around in her belly. "Stunning? I wouldn't go as far as to say that."

Lucifer looked almost hurt by her response. "You should. You are positively ethereal, and I feel honored that you would even have me in your presence. There is nothing more I would like to do right now than to kiss you and tell you how much you enchant me."

LUCIFER

Chloe couldn't believe the words coming from this man's mouth. This incredibly attractive man sat here telling her that he thought she was the sexiest thing alive and that he wanted to kiss her?

How could this be possible?

"You... you want to kiss me? Already?" Chloe sputtered, utterly stunned.

Lucifer nodded sincerely. "Nothing would make me happier. I can hardly control myself around you; you're just so... stunning."

That made Chloe giggle, but also because she suddenly felt so nervous. Were they really about to kiss this quickly into their first date?

"Well, I... I wouldn't say no to a kiss,"

Chloe said shyly, looking up at Lucifer under her lashes. When their eyes met, Lucifer looked like he had been hit by a train, but in a good way.

"Really?" he asked.

Chloe nodded, moisture dampening her panties underneath the miniskirt and heat filling her cheeks as she scented her own rush of desire, praying Lucifer didn't catch the unmistakable aroma the way her wolf senses did. "I would love that."

It seemed that was all Lucifer needed to hear. He shuffled around the booth so he sat right next to Chloe. He stared deeply into her eyes and cupped the bottom of her cheek, tilting her lips up toward his.

Chloe's heart hammered away in her

LUCIFER

chest. She couldn't believe this was just about to happen.

And then, it did.

Lucifer tilted his head to the right and gently pressed his lips over hers. The moment their lips touched, it felt like fireworks went off inside of Chloe. She had never felt this way when she'd kissed any guy ever before. It felt a bit like a key sliding into the right lock—it just fit the way it should and felt perfect.

As they kissed more, Chloe realized that Lucifer smelled and tasted like warm cinnamon. A pleasant smoky background smell she couldn't really identify tickled her nostrils. She very much enjoyed the combination wafting off the man. Feeling brave, Chloe wrapped her arm around Lucifer's neck and pulled herself in closer to him while she flicked her tongue inside his mouth. She could have imagined it because it was so quiet but she could have sworn she heard him groan in pleasure. That delighted Chloe, as did kissing him in general.

When they finally broke apart, both panting, Chloe couldn't help but giggle as Lucifer stared at her adoringly.

"See?" Lucifer said. "Ethereal."

They both chuckled, and then Chloe didn't know what more to say. She was so flustered by the kiss, and her brazen reaction to Lucifer' touch, that her mind suddenly went blank. She completely forgot how to have a first date conversation.

They sat there in pleasant silence for

LUCIFER

a few minutes. Chloe still had an incredibly hard time believing this hot guy found her so attractive when she could barely stand to look at herself in the morning. She felt that he was way out of her league, and had he not continued reassuring her that he thought she was absolutely stunning, she would have thought he was teasing her.

Finally, Lucifer took a long swig of his drink, his gaze once more roving over Chloe head to toe, and then he broke the silence. "You said you were a detective, is that right?"

Chloe nodded. "A homicide detective, or rather a special agent now. Basically, I work all of the cases that stump the other detectives... which, in the LAPD, is pretty often."

Lucifer chuckled and took another drink. "And do you find that being a wolf shifter helps or hinders you in your job?"

"Definitely helps," Chloe responded, taking a quick swig of her sunset colored drink. "All of my senses are heightened because of my shifting, which means I'm able to pick up on a lot more stuff than the others can even hope to. I've actually gotten a bit of a reputation around the department as the 'sensing' girl. One time, I was able to detect a supposedly odorless poison in tomato soup from the next room over."

Lucifer looked highly amused, and then laughed. "I never thought about it that way. I figured it would be very challenging to be a shifter and a

LUCIFER

homicide detective, because you might be tempted to shift more frequently. Is your shifting trigger anger? I know that's how it is for a lot of other shifters."

Chloe nodded. "You've got it. It does get a bit distracting sometimes when I get frustrated at a crime scene or when I'm interrogating a suspect or something, but it isn't that bad. I'll just excuse myself, go for a little shift-n-run, and then come back to the scene. I had to do that at my most recent case, actually."

Lucifer looked very interested. "Would you mind telling me about your latest case? Are you even allowed to do that?"

"I can tell you a bit, but you're right," Chloe confirmed. "I'm not allowed to tell you all that much."

She then launched into a retelling of

what she was allowed to mention to Lucifer about the most recent murder. She told him about the strange art on the wall, the way the body had been found, and she even talked a bit about how she saw similarities between herself and the victim.

"And that's why my best friend, Heidi, actually suggested that I come to the speed dating," Chloe finished her story. "Well, actually, that's why Heidi forced me to come to speed dating. I... may have been a bit reluctant to come the first time, and then convincing me to come back was damn near impossible." She chuckled.

Lucifer bellowed out a deep baritone laugh upon hearing that. Chloe really liked the way his laugh sounded, and when he smiled, it made his whole face light up. She could very much get used to seeing his smiling face more often.

"I, for one, am very grateful that you decided to come back for a second night," Lucifer said, putting the palms of his hands on top of the table.

Chloe smiled at him. She wanted to say that she was glad she'd come, too, but she still felt a little shy in this sexy-as-sin man's presence. But then, oddly, she was overcome by a sudden surge of confidence and decided to throw caution to the wind and to take a chance.

"I'm really glad that I came too," she said quietly, her gaze on her fingers twisting in her lap.

When Chloe looked up at Lucifer, he was gazing at her with such intensity, she felt as though he looked right into her soul. They stared at each other like that for a minute, and then Lucifer finally broke his gaze away, a growl rumbling from his throat.

"In that case," he said in a deep, rather seductive voice, "what would you say to going on a proper date, just the two of us? I have a few ideas in mind, if you'd like me to suggest locations."

Chloe sat silent for a moment, pondering. She felt extremely hesitant to go on a second date with anyone after her disastrous first three dates with people from the DeLux Cafe. However, she liked the sense she got of this guy, the way he felt made her head spin and her panties wet, after all. She could only hope against hope that if they did go out,

LUCIFER

the date would be a whole lot better than her first three.

What's the worst that could happen?

If it goes badly, I've already got practice in getting out of dates quickly.

This would be no problem, right?

Chloe finally nodded, flashing Lucifer a playful smile. "I'd like that very much. What are your suggestions?"

A wide grin spread across Lucifer's handsome face, and it made Chloe's insides do a somersault.

"More like what *aren't* my suggestions," Lucifer joked. "We could go to Venice beach, walk around and dip our toes in the water. We could take a drive out to Beverly Hills and pretend to be as rich as anyone who lives there. We could go down to Rodeo Drive and I could buy you something as beautiful as you are. We could go to the Getty and—"

"Oh the Getty, yes!" Chloe interrupted him, her excitement palpable. "I've lived in LA for so long and I've never had an excuse to go. I hear it's one of the most beautiful art museums in the world."

Lucifer nodded appreciatively. "You have excellent taste, Chloe. The Getty is what I would prefer to suggest as my personal favorite out of everything, too. Shall I pick you up at your apartment say… tomorrow afternoon at one?"

Chloe's eyes widened. "Tomorrow? Isn't that a bit soon?"

Lucifer shrugged and said in a gravelly voice that sent chills down her spine, "If it were all up to me, we would never leave each other's sight ever again."

The comment made Chloe giggle once more. A girl could get used to this. The compliments and slightly possessive nature Lucifer exuded made her heart thump behind her breast and she clamped her thighs together to ward off the tingling heat she felt building. "Well, in that case, I think tomorrow should be just fine. If you'd like to give me your phone number, I'll text you my address."

Lucifer immediately pulled out his phone and the two of them exchanged numbers. After that, he kept looking at his phone like he was waiting for something. Eventually, he glanced up at her and said, "Are you going to send it to me?"

"Oh, I was going to do that

tomorrow," Chloe said nonchalantly.

Lucifer raised an eyebrow at her and growled out, "What, do you not trust me with your address tonight?"

Chloe laughed. "No, no, it'll just be easier that way. Thank you for tonight, Lucifer, it was nice meeting you."

Chloe extended her hand for him to shake. Lucifer looked down at her hand, a peculiar hurt expression crossing his features. But he grasped her and shook it, and then, in a very smooth move, he used their connection to pull Chloe toward him. Holding her pressed firmly to his chest, Lucifer gazed deeply into her eyes and Chloe felt like she just wanted to melt into his arms.

"Chloe Frost," he whispered, his dark eyes clearly rimmed with a scarlet glow

LUCIFER

now, "you have enchanted me heart and soul. Thank you for tonight."

And then, he put his hand on her cheek, tilted her chin upward toward him and brushed his lips across hers. It was just as magnificent at the first kiss and made Chloe weak in the knees. This time, however, the taste of warm cinnamon had stronger undertones of smoky spice to it, almost like a burnt whisky or something she still couldn't place, but she decided she liked the flavor of him very much.

Chloe didn't want it to ever stop tasting Lucifer and feeling the way she did in his arms, safe and secure yet desired and filled with longing. But she knew it was already starting to get late and, unfortunately, she had work in the morning. And so at long last, Chloe pulled away from the kiss and quickly grabbed her bag so that she wouldn't be tempted to stay with him any longer. She shuffled out of the booth, stood up, and then finally looked back at him.

When their eyes met, Chloe suddenly realized something; in all of their conversation that night, she hadn't ever asked what sort of paranormal creature lay under the man's exterior. Curiosity getting the better of her, she stared at him a moment longer, trying to discern it for herself, a glimpse of dark, red-rimmed eyes passing through her mind, until she decided that she couldn't figure it out.

"I realized I never asked you," Chloe inquired, "what are you other than

LUCIFER

human? Shifter? Demon? I've tried to figure it out but I just can't."

A satisfied smile crept across Lucifer's face. "Oh, Chloe. Haven't you been able to tell by now that I'm so much more than a mere mortal? I'll reveal all to you on our date tomorrow."

Chloe opened her mouth to respond, slightly annoyed at his attempt at an air of mystery after she'd laid all her cards on the table for him earlier, but then she decided to just smile at him and slipped through the curtains and out into the main room of DeLux.

What a mysterious guy.

But I suppose he's right, I can figure all of that out when we meet tomorrow.

CHAPTER SIXTEEN

WHEN LUCIFER WOKE up the next morning in his apartment, he couldn't stop smiling. It was a very new sensation to him, because he had always been so serious. But now, he had a woman who he was going to seduce and make his own, and the thought of that was utterly intoxicating.

LUCIFER

Lucifer spent his day prior to going to meet with Chloe going about his usual tasks. He checked in with Ash, the General of the Daemonium Guard, about how things were going down in Purgatory. He ravenously ate his lunch, his thoughts filled with Chloe the entire time, and then took Fenriz for a long walk. The hellhound was never really happy to be on earth in his Chihuahua form, but he did enjoy the long walk and so that kept him happy. Of course, Lucifer could hardly concentrate on much of anything with the prospect of his date with Chloe happening that afternoon so he felt like he'd done the entire walk in a complete daze.

Around an hour before he was set to pick her up, Chloe texted him her address. She didn't live too far from him, which was convenient, but he still wanted to leave plenty of time. It would be his worst nightmare to be late for such a much anticipated date.

Right before he had to leave, Lucifer slipped into what he considered to be his 'seduction outfit': he wore a well-fitting, expensive black t-shirt, a pair of his best dark jeans, and his best black boots. He wasn't sure if he should do something different with his hair, but there wasn't really much he could do with it anyway. In the end, he decided that he was satisfied the way it looked, the slightly curled, dark raven locks looked silky and shiny, and complimented his skin tone perfectly, after all. Flashing his reflection a brilliant mega-watt smile, he turned on

LUCIFER

his heel and strode out the door.

Lucifer hopped into his convertible and put the roof down, hoping Chloe would be impressed by it. No, scratch that—he knew she would be. It was a beautiful car, she was a beautiful woman—it was a match made in heaven.

When Lucifer pulled up outside of her apartment complex, he wasn't sure what step to take next. His indecision was perplexing and most definitely out of character.

Would it be best to text her and let her know he was here?

Should he buzz up to her apartment to let her know that he'd arrived?

Or should he just wait in the car, as they had decided on a time to meet out front earlier?

GINA KINCADE & ERZABET BISHOP

It turned out Lucifer didn't actually have to make any decision. By the time he'd turned off the car, checked his appearance once more in the rearview mirror, and then looked up, he saw Chloe coming out of her building. She looked even more beautiful than she had the other night. Today she wore a pretty yellow, strappy summer dress that billowed in the wind as it blew, accompanied by a pair of pale yellow, high-heeled sandals that only emphasized the length of her legs. The accessories made Lucifer practically drool to imagine those heels digging into his ass when Chloe wrapped those delicious limbs around his waist. Her hair appeared incredibly majestic; the silvery-white, long strands glimmered in the sunshine like they were embedded with diamonds. As soon as Lucifer saw her, he wanted to skip the whole date and just take her right that moment.

He knew that wouldn't be a good idea, though, so he forced control on himself, pushing down the desire thrumming through his veins and adjusting the throbbing manhood that pressed against his zipper. He concentrated on the least sexy things he could think of: tuna salad, going to the dentist, and doing taxes. Unfortunately, not even the thought of trying to find the right tax form could make him any less aroused.

You're behaving like a virgin on his first date!

Get it together, old chap!

Chloe walked up to the car and gave him a big, friendly wave and a welcoming smile.

"Hi, Lucifer!" she said cheerily, opening the car door and climbing into the car. "Wow, what a ride! This makes my car look like a scrap mobile."

Lucifer chuckled. "You like it? I hoped you would. You look… magnificent."

Lucifer and Chloe looked into each other's eyes, and then without saying anything, Lucifer took her by the chin and placed a butterfly-soft kiss on her lips. Chloe seemed surprised at first, but then she sank into it, tangling her hands in his t-shirt. She slid her hand over his chest, around his shoulder, threading her fingers through the silky hair at the back of his head, and allowed a moan to slip from her throat. They kissed for a long time, the anticipation of what Lucifer had planned for later only escalating and making his cock ache more than it had before.

Finally, Lucifer drew back, panting hard, and flashed her a wicked smile. "You ready to go? Or should we just stay here for the rest of the day?" A chuckle reverberated in his chest.

Chloe giggled and shook her head. "While that does sound tempting," she said, her voice breathy, "I have really been looking forward to going to the Getty. So, let's go!"

Lucifer did as he was told and put the pedal to the metal. The drive to the Getty shouldn't have taken too long, but in Los Angeles traffic, it took a while. Lucifer and Chloe chatted back and forth about insignificant things at first: how her job was evolving, her friendship with someone named Mackenzie, Lucifer's time at the cafe. But as they got closer to the museum, Lucifer could hardly control himself, he was so enamored and aroused by the beautiful young woman sitting next to him. At one point while Chloe was talking about the case she was working on right now, Lucifer decided to be bold and put his hand on her leg. The moment his fingertips touched her skin, he knew there would be no going back from this when that simple little touch sent sparks of pleasure thrumming across his nerves and down to his cock.

Her leg was warm to the touch, and a

nice contrast to his ice-cold digits. Chloe stopped speaking and sucked in a sharp breath, looking down at her leg.

"You like that?" Lucifer asked her, his gravelly voice laced with lust.

She nodded, her brows drawing together. "Mhmm," she said, biting her lip, "but the sizzling zap I just got from your fingers traveled to places I truly didn't expect!" She chuckled nervously and swept her lashes downward as a pink color filled her cheeks.

Emotion surged in his heart, filling it to bursting. "Thrilled to hear it's not just me." He grinned and sucked in a breath. He had to remind himself to keep his eyes on the road, otherwise he might lose his concentration entirely.

Thankfully, before he could get too

lost in his fantasy about Chloe, they pulled up to the Getty. They found a good parking space and then got on the small train to take it to the museum. As they sat side-by-side in the tiny train car, Lucifer could hardly keep his mind on the museum. All he wanted to do was take her home and claim her.

When they did arrive at the museum, however, Lucifer was smitten by the way Chloe became fascinated and stared in awe at every painting they saw. They wandered the place for hours, taking everything in and even stopping at the outdoor cafe to get something to eat. The more Chloe talked about her passion for art, the deeper Lucifer fell in love with her. He loved her passion and her knowledge, and hoped that would continue as they pursued their relationship.

After lunch, they continued looking at the works of art. When they stood in front of Van Gogh's *Irises*, Chloe was practically moved to tears. He'd never seen anyone get so emotional in front of a painting, and it only endeared her to him more.

By five-thirty, they had toured the whole place. Lucifer decided it was time to make his move.

"So, what do you feel like doing now?" he asked casually as they strolled out of the gift shop. Chloe had bought a postcard set of Van Gogh's works as well as a poster from one of the other exhibits. She looked at him shyly.

"Well..." she said, flashing him a

smile, her words coming out in a sultry tone that greatly pleased Lucifer. She pressed her body against his, raising herself up on her tiptoes and pressing a kiss on the corner of his mouth. "I thought you might enjoy coming to my apartment. We could order some food, put on a movie... see where the night takes us?"

Lucifer could feel his eyes flash red with excitement, but he did his best to control himself. He raised his hand to the side of her face and slid his fingers over her cheekbone. "That sounds perfect. Dinner will be... my treat." He winked at her and Chloe blushed. He knew that it was going to be a good evening.

The ride home was agonizingly long.

LUCIFER

The traffic now made the traffic earlier look like child's play, but Lucifer supposed that was what he got for trying to travel during rush hour.

After what seemed like an eternity, they pulled up in front of Chloe's building. Lucifer parked his car somewhere he knew it wouldn't get ticketed or towed on the off chance that he decided to stay there overnight, which he hoped he would. They held hands as they walked up the four floors of stairs, and when Chloe unlocked her door, Lucifer's heart was absolutely pounding in his chest. He couldn't wait to get his hands on her.

When she opened the door, Lucifer was thoroughly impressed by her decor.

"You've got a great place," he

complimented her.

"Thank you," she said. "I've worked pretty hard on it, but I still don't quite feel like it's perfect yet. It's just missing something."

Lucifer chuckled and was just about to respond when a small cat trotted out of the bedroom and came to rub itself against Chloe's legs. The young woman bent down and scooped up the feline. Lucifer was not a big fan of cats, and he was immediately worried how this little thing would get along with Fenriz, but he still smiled warmly at it.

"This is Atticus," Chloe introduced the cat, petting its head fondly. "He's a lovely boy, but he's not too big of a fan of men, so I wouldn't recommend trying to pet him for at least a little while."

LUCIFER

"Sure," Lucifer said, looking the cat in the eye. "I'll just admire him from afar, then."

Chloe laughed and returned the cat to the floor. "Speaking of which," she said, turning back and looking at Lucifer from under her lowered lashes. Her tongue darted out to lick her lips, and she continued, "You don't have to keep admiring me from afar. You were so well behaved all afternoon... Would you put your hands on me now?"

Lucifer was stunned. He'd never thought he'd hear Chloe talk like this, but he felt utterly overjoyed that she felt comfortable enough to tell him what she desired. His voice thick with lust, he replied, "I thought you'd never ask. I'd be delighted to put my hands on you,

Chloe."

He took a step forward, grasped her by the waist, and drew her in close. Lucifer raised his hand to the side of her face to cup her cheek. He slid the pad of his thumb up over her cheekbone, and lowered his mouth to hers. Chloe made a buzzing sound against his lips that sounded like a growl, and Lucifer could feel their connection growing stronger. She parted her lips to moan and his tongue slipped into her mouth, taking the kiss deeper, devouring her. She pressed herself flush against his body, wrapping her arms around his neck, and his hot, pulsing erection pressed against his zipper, straining to be free.

Lucifer knew if they kept going, he was going to claim her right here and

LUCIFER

now. He needed to pull himself out of it; she deserved far more than a quick romp on the livingroom floor. He took a step back, his breaths coming hard, and took her hand, lifting the digits to his lips.

"Chloe," he said in a deep, raspy voice. "There's something I've known about you from the moment we met, but I needed to know if you felt it, too. And, if you do, I need to know if you believe in it."

Chloe looked up at him with her big, innocent eyes and smiled. "Yes, Lucifer? What is it?"

Lucifer cleared his throat and sucked in a deep breath. "Chloe, the moment I laid eyes on you, I knew you were my fated mate. I've searched my whole life for the person who I'm meant to be with for all eternity, which for someone like me is several millennia, and now you've finally arrived. I know without a doubt that I am ready to completely give myself over to you, but I need to know if you feel the same way. So... do you?"

Chloe looked away from Lucifer, and he immediately worried that he'd spoken too soon.

You should have waited.

You're scaring her.

You should've stayed calm!

But then, Chloe gave him one of her most charming smiles.

"Well," Chloe said, biting her bottom lip, "I know that when I saw you, I felt like I'd been struck by lightning. Does that mean that we're fated mates?"

Lucifer was practically overwhelmed

LUCIFER

with joy. "Yes, it does. That's exactly how it felt for me, too. I haven't been able to get you out of my mind since we met, Chloe."

"I haven't been able to either," Chloe said sweetly. "But Lucifer, there's so much I don't know about you. You haven't even told me what sort of paranormal being you are!"

Lucifer could have slapped himself. He couldn't believe he hadn't told her that yet. He quickly decided what he should reveal and what he should hold back: he was going to tell her about being a demon, but not yet inform her that he was the leader of the Underworld.

"You're absolutely right, Chloe, and I'm sorry for my error," he apologized. "I should have told you right away. But to make things right, can I show you right now?"

Chloe's eyes widened and she nodded slowly.

Lucifer was thrilled that she allowed him to transform right in front of her. He closed his eyes for a moment, concentrated on his other being, and then quickly felt himself beginning to transform with ease. He became much taller and broader, his skin tone appeared slightly redder, and he could feel his wings expanding out of his back. He didn't have horns, but he did have two tiny protrusions in his forehead that made him look even more demonic than some of the lesser demons. He opened his eyes, knowing they would appear full

LUCIFER

on crimson now, and watched the awe in Chloe's face as he flapped his wings a few times to get them to their full expansion and then stood in front of her.

She didn't say anything for a long time. She just stood there with her jaw open, absolutely stunned by his transformation. Lucifer deeply hoped he hadn't terrified her, and also that she felt comfortable with this form, as he was very comfortable in it. He contemplated mentioning his status once more, but Chloe interrupted him.

"You're..." she began, but then trailed off. "You're a demon?"

Lucifer nodded slowly. "Yes, I am. I live down in Purgatory when I'm not here working at the cafe."

"Wow," Chloe whispered, looking

impressed. She took a step toward him and, lifted her hand to gently run her fingers across the protrusions in his forehead. Your wings are... magnificent. May I touch them?"

Lucifer nodded emphatically. He loved it when women touched his wings. There was something about a woman's touch on them that was so arousing. It almost felt better than doing the deed itself.

Almost.

Chloe slid her hand down the side of his face, over his chest, around his shoulder, and finally reached out and gingerly stroked her digits down the edge of Lucifer's black wings, coming to a stop at the tip of crimson on one feather. It felt so good that it sent a shiver down his spine and he groaned.

"You can be... rougher, if you'd like," he growled at her.

Chloe gave him a wicked smile and added more pressure to her caresses. It felt so good that Lucifer had to remind himself not to just bite her and claim her right now. He had to wait until she said yes. He exhaled a long, shaky breath.

Chloe took another step toward him and pressed herself right up against him. Lucifer caught a whiff of her irresistible sweet cherry and cool morning air scent and brought his hands up to cup either side of her face.

"I love that you're a demon," Chloe said breathlessly. "I think it's... very sexy."

Lucifer arched an eyebrow and

grinned. "Oh, do you?"

Chloe nodded and flashed him a divine smile. "I certainly do. It's so enticing that I... Well, I want to get closer to you."

That was all it took for Lucifer to let go of his hesitation and allow his libido to go into overdrive. He gazed down into her glittering, ice blue eyes, more beautiful than any precious jewel imaginable. Cupping her face, he tilted his head and captured her lips with his once more.

Chloe growled low in her throat and flung her arms around his neck. Each swipe of her tongue against his, each roll of her hips against his manhood, caused the heat in his nerve endings to overflow. The urge to unwrap her made his fingers

LUCIFER

tremble and itch.

He moved one hand down from her waist to cup her ass, pulling her tight against him, and then leaned down to scoop her up with both hands, wrapping her legs around his waist.

Everything moved so furiously fast and Lucifer had to retract his wings more quickly than he ever had before to get through the doorway. It hurt a bit to do it so rapidly, but it was worth it. He was finally going to be with his fated mate. Chloe's body pressed against his felt like heaven, especially since all he'd ever known was Purgatory. They continued exploring each other's bodies and allowing their passion to build up. Lucifer took control at one point and Chloe let him do whatever he wanted to her. The arousal was intoxicating and Lucifer didn't ever want to stop.

He backed them into the bedroom amid their combined growls and groans, pressing his mouth to her throat. Turning around, he laid her on the bed and hovered over her, resting his weight on his elbows. Divesting them both of their clothing with one flick of his wrist, he brought his mouth down on her breast, delighting in the hiss of breath she sucked in through her teeth.

He kneaded her other breast with his large, warm hand, rolling her hardened nipple between his thick fingers, his teeth grazing the other. Grabbing his broad shoulders, she moaned and squeezed her thighs together. He wedged them apart with his legs and trailed kisses all the way down her ribcage. Lucifer growled hungrily as he moved his way down to her belly button, pausing to dip his tongue in the crevasse as Chloe bucked her hips and squealed, her hands alternately gripping his shoulders, her nails digging into the hard flesh, and then caressing the contours of his back with the pads of her fingertips.

Lucifer stared up at her though eyes clouded with red. His voice thick with lust, he asked, "Chloe, what do you want?"

She threaded her fingers though his hair and squeezed the nape of his neck. "Your mouth. I need your tongue," she panted, bucking her hips.

"Then you shall have it." He parted

her thighs and groaned. Everything about you is divine. I love that you're so responsive," he growled, the corners of his lips curved into a smile. He lowered himself to her exposed sex and trailed a slow line with his tongue from her opening to her engorged clit. "You are delicious," he groaned, licking her honey from his lips. He held her legs in place with his large hands, devouring her sex with open-mouthed kisses as her muscles spasmed and clenched.

"Lucifer, please… I need…" she cried out, her hips roving back and forth, her hands pressing his head to the apex of her thighs.

He nodded, growling, and murmured against her skin, "Yes, my love, I know what you need. And you shall have it! "

LUCIFER

He wrapped his lips around her clit and sucked, pressing a thick finger into her welcoming heat, and continued his relentless onslaught until she cried out, every limb on her body trembling through her climax.

As her breathing slowed and she lay satisfied and boneless, he kissed a trail back up her body and settled his hips between her thighs. By the time their eyes met, he gazed at her through a vivid deep scarlet haze, nearly at the height of his passion. He placed a butterfly-soft kiss on her lips as she gazed back at him through heavy-lidded eyes, the love and desire shining in her eyes making his breath quicken. As he ground his thick length against her clit, she clung to his broad back, panting, moaning, mewling, and squirming with desire. He lined up the blunt tip of his erection against her opening. She felt so hot and slick, so ready. He shuddered in anticipation, his cock throbbing and straining toward the heat radiating from her sex.

"Chloe," he whispered, his voice barely a croak, "I have to know before we go any further... Will you let me claim you? Will you vow to be mine forever?"

Chloe's face contorted with pleasure, her breathing once again increasing, and she looked him in the eyes. There was a momentary pause, and then, in between her irresistible growling and purring noises and her rolling hip movements as she ground herself against his hardness, she sucked in a deep breath.

LUCIFER

"Yes," she said, her eyes glittering. "Yes, please claim me!"

She slid her hands down to his ass and dug her fingers into the hard flesh of his glutes, tilting her hips up toward him.

Lucifer growled loudly, "You are perfection. And all mine." He filled her, sheathing himself to the hilt in her heat, hissing as her hot channel clamped around his thick, throbbing member. He peppered her face with soft kisses as her muscles throbbed and adjusted around his girth.

"Yours," she repeated.

He began entering and withdrawing from her slippery channel with shallow thrusts. "I love how we fit so perfectly."

"Lucifer... " She clamped her legs

around him, digging the nails of her fingers into his tight globes, making him hiss through his teeth.

In and out he went, back and forth, deeper and deeper, building up to a rhythm that had her crying out and writhing, moving her hips in counterpoint to his thrusts.

Lost in their shared passion, their pleasure, she threw back her head and howled as her muscles clamped around him, her climax tipping her over the edge and sending his own rushing to a peak.

He continued thrusting into her, the rush of ecstasy as he pumped into her more addictive than anything he'd ever experienced. He drew out the sensations until his vision turned blood red and white-hot pleasure raced along his every

LUCIFER

nerve from his spine to his balls. With a roar, he shuddered his climax inside her, his teeth piercing the skin of her shoulder, her life force coating the inside of his mouth. At that moment, he felt a connection to her that was hotter than hellfire, deeper than the darkest sea, stronger than the biggest tidal wave, and he knew he would never let her go. A feeling of possessiveness he'd never known lodged in his heart and mind as he licked over the wounds in her skin, sealing them with his saliva.

Chloe was his.

Forever.

Mine! His beast howled.

CHAPTER SEVENTEEN

WHEN CHLOE WOKE up the next morning in her bed with Lucifer lying beside her, it took her a moment to remember what had happened the day before. She easily remembered their afternoon at the Getty and how happy she had been touring the museum on his arm, and then they'd come home

LUCIFER

and...

Oh.

Oh my.

Chloe sat bolt upright, clutching the sheets to her bare breasts. She was so surprised by herself; she couldn't believe she had let this demon claim her! She had to think about the mixed emotions, sort them out, and figure out where she stood on this unexpected development.

Did she regret agreeing to let him claim her?

No, she decided she did not. She'd never felt about anyone the way she felt about Lucifer. But she couldn't believe that she had just up and decided to be with this man for the rest of her life. This was the most impulsive thing that she had ever done... but it thrilled her.

GINA KINCADE & ERZABET BISHOP

Chloe looked down at Lucifer sprawled out across her bed, his soft snores making her giggle. A small smile crept across her lips, and she was so excited just by the sight of him. He was handsome, kind, generous... and a bit dominating, but she liked that about him. He was a very exciting man, not to mention sexy-as-sin, and the fact that he was a demon comfortable in his other skin only made him more attractive. Chloe felt very elated that she had given in to her baser instincts and decided to be intimate with him, but still a few of the usual doubts and insecurities remained in her mind.

She immediately pushed them from her mind, however, when Lucifer opened his dark eyes, looked up at her, and

LUCIFER

flashed that brilliant, mega-watt smile. Chloe lay back down beside him and he slipped his arm around her waist.

"Good morning, my sexy wolf," he said with a wicked grin on his face. "You were nothing short of extraordinary last night."

Chloe giggled and pulled herself in closer to him, resting her head on his chest where she could hear the steady thrum of his heartbeat in her ear. "Oh yeah? You weren't too bad yourself, Lucifer!" She tilted her face up to his, met his eyes, eyes that shone with love, and grinned.

He chuckled and pulled her into his chest, wrapping his arms around her back. His large hand rubbed gentle circles on her back, and she melted into him, content to simply lie there in his warm embrace.

Chloe loved the feeling of his big strong arms around her, and every time she would remember that he was also a demon, a jolt of excitement would run through her.

Lucifer pressed his lips to the top of her head and said, "Would you like to come see my apartment today? Just for, you know, a change of scenery?"

Chloe nodded enthusiastically. "I would love that. Shall we make breakfast and then go?"

Lucifer chuckled and shook his head, pulling her in toward him. "Make breakfast? No. That takes far too long and is far too much effort. I'm taking you out for breakfast... and lunch... and then

LUCIFER

I'm having you for dinner."

Between each meal in the list, Lucifer peppered her cheeks with light kisses, and when he completed the sentiment, he grabbed her ass and pulled her hips in to press against his hardness.

She giggled and squealed, grinding her pubis against his. "Hmmm. I like the sound of that, she murmured against his heated skin, her growly voice reverberating through his chest and tickling her cheek. He lifted her chin with a finger, tilted his head down, and lavished her with a kiss so deep it made her toes curl. His tongue caressed and teased hers with strokes she swore she could feel across every erogenous zone. Chloe wasn't sure exactly what the day would hold for them, but whatever he had planned, she felt eager to experience it with him.

After they were finally able to pull themselves out of bed, Chloe dumped enough food for the rest of the day in Atticus' bowl, just to be safe, she figured, and freshened the water in his cat fountain. Then, they quickly showered together, dressed, and traipsed out the door a few minutes later.

Lucifer drove them to the Neptune Cafe that was halfway between his place and hers. Chloe had never heard of it before, but as she looked over the menu, she saw that it was one of the most expensive places she'd ever eaten at.

"Lucifer," she whispered, "I think this place might be too fancy for me!"

But Lucifer just chuckled and shook

his head as he continued looking over the menu. "It most certainly isn't, my dear. Choose anything you'd like, it's on me."

Chloe still wasn't convinced that she should have been eating at as fine an establishment as this one, but eventually, she made a decision. She ordered the Belgian waffles with an array of exotic fruits, most of which she had never heard of. When it arrived, it was piled so high that Chloe was convinced she would never be able to finish all of it. However, when she saw how swiftly and hungrily Lucifer ate, she knew that she didn't have to worry about wasting any food.

After breakfast, they drove to Lucifer's apartment. When they pulled up, Chloe immediately felt impressed by the stunning red brick exterior and immaculately groomed grounds with wrought iron gates framing the long, triple-wide driveway. She gawked at the beautiful old building; the kind one would see an old Hollywood movie star living in and, of course, looked like something that Chloe would never be able to afford.

"Wow," she whispered as they pulled into Lucifer's parking spot, "this place is amazing. How can you afford a place like this? No offense."

The moment the words were out of Chloe's mouth, she regretted it.

Why did you have to ask that?
That's so rude!

But Lucifer just laughed and flashed

LUCIFER

her his trademark brilliant smile. "I'll tell you a bit later. It's my biggest secret."

Chloe was intrigued but did not press him any more on the subject. They strode inside, rode silently up the elevator hand in hand, and when Lucifer opened the door to his penthouse apartment, Chloe gasped.

It was the most beautiful apartment she'd ever seen. Absolutely massive and sprawling, framed on three sides by floor to ceiling windows, allowing natural sunlight to fill the room, it looked as though it had been decorated by a professional interior designer. The walls were all painted an elegant eggshell white/grey mixture, and all of the stylish furniture was clearly handcrafted dark, polished wood. The cushions on the couch were a deep maroon soft leather, and Chloe got the sense that Lucifer liked colors and textures that aroused him.

"You like it?" Lucifer asked, throwing his keys on the counter of his massive kitchen.

Chloe nodded slowly. "How could I not? This place is amazing! I can't believe this is yours! You're sure you're not just borrowing this from a friend to impress me?"

Lucifer chuckled and shook his head. "No, sadly not. This is all mine."

Right then, a small dog came trotting out of the bedroom and started yapping at them. Chloe instantly melted.

"You didn't tell me you have a dog!" she exclaimed. "He's adorable! What's

LUCIFER

his name?"

"This is Fenriz," Lucifer introduced the Chihuahua, picking him up and bringing him over to her. "He may not seem like it, but he packs a big bite."

Chloe chuckled, thinking he must be joking. But just in case he wasn't, she let the dog sniff her finger before petting him. The dog looked initially reluctant, but then allowed Chloe to pet him. His tail wagged very hard as he stared up at her through large brown eyes.

"Chloe," Lucifer said, and set the dog down. "There's something more I need to tell you."

"Is it the big secret that you were telling me about in the car?" she asked, tilting her head to meet his gaze.

Lucifer nodded. "It most certainly is,

and I need to tell you now because I think it will affect our relationship going forward."

Chloe nodded. "Please, go ahead."

"You see," Lucifer said, taking her hand and staring deeply into her eyes. "I'm not just any demon, Chloe. I'm... I'm the king of the Underworld, and I spend a great deal of time down in my castle in Purgatory. That's how I manage to afford an apartment of this magnitude, and that's how I ended up with a hellhound like Fenriz."

A shocked breath whistled through her teeth. Chloe nodded, letting his words sink in. She looked down at the tiny little dog. "That's... a hellhound? I always thought they were bigger!"

Lucifer chuckled and Fenriz gave

LUCIFER

Chloe a little growl. "Easy boy, easy. He is much bigger when we're down in Purgatory, but he always takes this form when we're on earth so he doesn't terrify the humans. It's actually very considerate of him."

She nodded, her brows drawing together. She chewed on the inside of her cheek. She was very surprised, but it didn't change how she felt about him. She still knew that she wanted to spend however long they had together... it would just make things a little more complicated.

"How does that make you feel, knowing that?" Lucifer asked her. A muscle in his jaw twitched.

"Well," Chloe began, and exhaled a long breath. "To tell you the truth, I don't know much about Purgatory, so I don't have a whole lot to say. But I know it doesn't change the way I feel about you, and I still want to be with you. The only problem is that... well, I don't want to leave earth. I'm very happy here. I have a wonderful job, a great life. What would this mean for our relationship?"

Lucifer became serious and took Chloe's hands. "Well, I do need to spend a good amount of time down in Purgatory, but I also know that you need to spend a lot of time up here for your job and your friends. I know we could work something out if we work on it together but... it would be an adjustment for the both of us."

Chloe nodded, looking deeply into Lucifer's eyes. "Lucifer, I... I know I said you could claim me, but I think that with this new information... I need some time to think. I know that I want to be with you, my fated mate, but I need to figure out how I'm going to feel about making such major changes to my life. Is that okay?"

Lucifer looked very disappointed, but only for a minute. His eyes softened and the corners of his lips curled into a smile. "Of course that's all right, my darling. You can take as long as you'd like to think it over. But until you decide, must we be apart?"

Chloe shook her head emphatically. "No, absolutely not! In fact, I was thinking... perhaps we could partake in the pleasures we indulged in last night again?"

Lucifer smiled mischievously at her. "You want to go again? Are you sure you can handle it so soon after last night?"

Chloe had never been so sure of anything in her life. "Yes. Absolutely. I want you to take me."

That was all that Chloe needed to say. Lucifer jumped into action, scooping her up and striding toward his bedroom.

Chloe couldn't get the knowledge that Lucifer would have to be away from her for so long out of her head. She didn't know exactly what she was going to do about their future, but she did know she was going to enjoy right now.

CHAPTER EIGHTEEN

WHEN THE SUN came up the next morning, Chloe silently crawled out of Lucifer's bed and quickly slipped back into her clothing from the day before. She needed some time to think on her own and didn't want to disturb him. He slept like a log, his soft snores filling the quiet room, and so Chloe wasn't really

LUCIFER

worried about waking him. Still, she tried to be as silent as she could.

When she'd made it out of the bedroom and was collecting her purse to get out the door, Chloe saw that Fenriz had come to say goodbye to her. She bent down to the little dog's level, let him sniff her hand again, and then gave him a few good scratches behind the ear.

"I'm sure you're much bigger and scarier when you're down in Purgatory," Chloe said to him. "But right now, you're pretty darn cute. I just hope you'll get along with my cat."

At the mention of the word cat, Fenriz took a step back and gave her a little growl, cocking his head to the side. Chloe took that as a bad sign and did not try to pet him again. She knew when to step back and make sure she didn't get bitten.

When Chloe got out into the street, she called a cab and headed back to her apartment. As the driver took her home, Chloe called Mackenzie. It rang three times before her friend picked up, clearly still very groggy so early in the morning.

"Why in the hell are you calling me so early? This had better be a life or death situation, otherwise I'm hanging up on you right now," Mackenzie said grumpily.

Chloe chuckled. "Sorry, Mackenzie. No, this isn't life or death... This is more life or afterlife."

She heard Mackenzie make a strange sound on the other end of the phone. "What? Did I hear that right?" the other woman barked.

Chloe then launched into a re-telling of everything that had happened in the last few days. Mackenzie was silent the whole time, which was an achievement for the boisterous woman.

"So now I don't know what to do—Thanks so much," Chloe said, handing the cash to the driver as she stepped back out into the street. "I mean, this guy is who I'm meant to be with, but do I really want to struggle through a long-distance relationship for the foreseeable future?"

"This... this is a problem I've never encountered before, I have to say," Mackenzie said sarcastically. "But it does seem like this fella is a keeper, and you shouldn't let your usual concerns about love keep you from being with him. I don't know, Chloe. I honestly don't think that the whole 'you here on earth' and 'him down in Purgatory' thing would be too big of a deal. I once dated a guy from Manchester for six months. We never met, but boy did we ever make it work!"

Chloe laughed as she walked up the flights of stairs to her apartment.

"I guess you're right," she admitted as she unlocked her door. "I'm just a bit hesitant because everything has felt like it's moved incredibly fast."

"That's valid," Mackenzie said truthfully. "But sometimes it's okay if things move at a faster pace than we'd like if it's right for us. Like with me and that guy from Manchester! He wanted to get my name tattooed on him and he wanted me to do the same. Now, of course, I knew it was a bad idea and that things were moving too fast for such a baby relationship. I'm really glad I went through with it now, though!"

Chloe unlocked the door to her apartment and replied, "Wait, why? You said you broke up with the guy, didn't you?"

"Mhmm," Mackenzie replied. "But now I have a really cool watercolor tattoo that I got to cover up the other one. I wouldn't have gotten that one if I hadn't done the other one in the first place!"

Chloe laughed out loud as she put down her purse. "Well, thanks for your suggestions, and for listening without judgment, as always, Mackenzie. I'll call you if there are any further developments."

"*If* there are any further developments?" Mackenzie screeched in disbelief. "More like *when* there are further developments! Chloe, honey, you've been waiting for a guy like this for... forever. If you lose him because you get scared of commitment, I'm going to come over there and launch you right the way down to Purgatory myself!"

They both laughed. Chloe promised to update her friend *when* there was a new development, and then they hung up. Just as she was sitting down on the couch to relax for a bit, Atticus came bounding out of the bedroom and she remembered she needed to feed him.

"Hello, Atticus boy!" she greeted him,

LUCIFER

extending her fingers for him to sniff like she always did. She expected him to do his usual—give it a quick sniff and then rub his face against her hand. But when he sniffed it, he did something he had never done before. He hissed at her.

Immediately, Chloe felt heartbroken. She couldn't understand why he was hissing at her.

"What's wrong, my love?" she asked him sweetly, but every step she took toward him he took a step backward. Chloe wracked her brain, trying to think of what might be upsetting him, until she finally realized what it was. She had petted Fenriz when she was over at Lucifer's house. Chloe chuckled in relief and washed her hands. When she extended her hand to him this time, he mashed his kitty face against her, just like he always did.

"Good boy," she said lovingly, and then went to fetch him his food.

Thank goodness!

I was so worried that him hissing at me right after I had returned from Lucifer's house was a bad omen.

But it was just the smell of the dog...

I think.

CHAPTER NINETEEN

WHEN LUCIFER WOKE up the morning after the incredible night he and Chloe had spent together, he rolled over expecting to embrace her and spend the morning with her, lazily and leisurely wake up with breakfast in bed, maybe a repeated performance of the intimacies of the night before. But when he realized

LUCIFER

that she wasn't there, he began to panic. He sat bolt upright and looked around the apartment to make sure she wasn't just in one of the other rooms. Before he let his imagination run away with him, he decided to check his phone and see if she had texted him.

Of course, she had.

"Good morning, sexy.

Thank you for last night... and the night before that. They were both heavenly. We have to be apart today as it's Heidi's baby shower, but also because I need a bit of time to think about our relationship. You know I feel very deeply for you, but I want to be absolutely certain we should be together before you claim me fully, and I you. I hope you have a wonderful day, and I'll call you tonight."

Lucifer re-read the text a few times to make sure he had read everything right. When he realized he hadn't missed anything, he was heartbroken. Chloe hadn't said outright that she wanted to end things between them because he was the ruler of the Underworld, but it certainly felt that way. Lucifer's thoughts started spiraling and he couldn't help thinking about what he would do if she didn't agree to let him claim her. He couldn't imagine his life without her, his fated mate, and if she didn't agree to be his... he wouldn't be able to go on.

Damn, what a pickle this has become!

Lucifer sat on the couch for a long

LUCIFER

time, unable to move. He didn't feel hungry, he didn't want to go to the cafe, even though he had a shift today. All he wanted to do was go crawl back into bed and sleep for a thousand years.

This wasn't like him. Usually when something disappointing happened to Lucifer, he became angry and would fight with everything with he had to in order to make the stars align for him. But this was a situation where he couldn't control things no matter how much he wanted to. He couldn't make his mate come to him and that perturbed him to no end. He just had to wait for her to see that they were made for each other. At least, he hoped she'd realize it. Sooner rather than later, preferably. Waiting, however, was the last thing Lucifer wanted to do right now.

At the time his shift was supposed to start, Lucifer's phone rang. He glanced down to the screen for a split second and saw that it was, of course, Aphrodite. He ignored it and lay back down on the couch, still utterly miserable. Aphrodite, however, was not one to just back down. She called him and called him and called him. Finally, on about the eighth call, Lucifer picked up.

"What?" he barked.

"Don't 'what' me, you ignorant demon," Aphrodite sputtered, sounding far angrier than he thought she would. "What the hell do you think you're doing? First of all, I can feel that the passion between you and your fated

LUCIFER

mate is draining. What's up with that? What did you do? And second of all, you were supposed to be here now! I've got a full cafe and no barista. Get yourself here in the next half hour or I'll never speak to you again."

Aphrodite hung up the phone before Lucifer could answer. He'd never heard her get this riled up before, so he worried she was truly upset about something and needed her friend. That made him anxious, worried about her, and so he quickly pulled on some work clothes and drove over there. He arrived within fifteen minutes, but when he got there, he didn't seek out Aphrodite. He knew she'd find him when she felt ready. He just went straight behind the drink counter and started serving drinks without his typical exuberant manner. He knew the patrons could tell, too.

When it came time for his break, he went out back to get some fresh air. However, Aphrodite waited there for him. She had her arms crossed in front of her chest and glared at him.

"So you did one thing I told you to do," she said. "But you haven't yet told me why the passion between you and Chloe is draining. Come on. Spill."

Lucifer sighed, his throat thickening with sorrow and pain, but did as she demanded. He explained all that had transpired between him and Chloe, right up to the text she left him that morning. When he finished, he expected some sort of sympathy from Aphrodite. She, however, did not look impressed.

LUCIFER

"So you're throwing a temper tantrum because the woman said she needed a day to think about spending *all eternity* with you when you've known each other for like... no time?" she asked him sarcastically. "My god. I thought you would have had a bit more faith than that, Lucifer."

"What do you mean?"

Aphrodite rolled her eyes. "What I mean is you've got to give her the day to herself to think things through. Don't you dare try to call her or text her or anything. She's going to be going over everything you've said to each other since you met to determine if she wants to be with you, which of course, she will. She's your fated mate, Lucifer. There couldn't be a better match than a demon and a white wolf. Just give her time and space."

Aphrodite gave him two pats on the shoulder and disappeared back into the cafe. Lucifer sighed rather pathetically, all the fight escaping him in an instant. He stood and looked out over the city from the balcony, mulling over what his long-time friend had said.

Time and space.

That's exactly what I don't want to give her right now. I want to be with her every minute of every hour of every day. But... if she needs to be absolutely sure she wants to be with me... then I guess, I'll just have to be patient.

CHAPTER TWENTY

AFTER CHLOE TOOK the morning to herself to think over what Lucifer had told her about being the ruler of the Underworld and living the majority of his time in Purgatory, she quickly got ready to go to Heidi's baby shower. She knew she couldn't be late or her best friend would kill her, so she didn't bother

LUCIFER

putting on much make up for the sake of time. She said goodbye to Atticus, giving him some chin scratches, and then headed over to Heidi and Dave's house.

On the drive there, however, Chloe couldn't get Lucifer off her mind. She knew he was her fated mate and they were perfect for each other, but she had such a hard time believing their relationship wouldn't remain long distance for... forever. She had no interest in moving down to Purgatory full-time, and it seemed that Lucifer had no interest in moving up to earth forever. If she had to leave, it would mean giving up her dream job, leaving all of her friends, family and everything she had ever known. Of course, there was always a possibility she might really end up liking living in Purgatory, but she couldn't know for sure until she got there, which made her very anxious.

When she tried to pull into the driveway of Heidi's house, however, Chloe was surprised to see there was an ambulance from the shifter hospital in the driveway. Suddenly, she no longer thought about Lucifer. She hastily parked the car, running inside to her friend.

When she threw open the door, however, Chloe had to immediately step aside. Two paramedics were carrying a panting, half-transformed Heidi on the stretcher. Her legs were in wolf form, but the top half of her body was still human. Chloe assumed that this was a side effect of the labor.

LUCIFER

"Ch-Chloe!" Heidi said between heavy breaths. "I'm so sorry, there's not going to be a baby shower but my water broke about— Uughhhhh!"

Heidi suddenly cried out in pain and the paramedics stopped moving her, placing her down on the driveway. Chloe came up beside her and grasped her hand while one of the paramedics tended to her.

"No apologies, no apologies!" Chloe said, trying not to sound panicked. "Your babies are coming, sweetheart! This is so exciting!" She flashed her best friend a smile.

Although Chloe tried to be enthusiastic, she actually felt terrified. Heidi's pregnancy as a shifter was already high-risk, but the fact that the babies were also half demons *and* there were twins in there, made this an extremely high-risk pregnancy. Heidi was meant to have a scheduled c-section at the shifter hospital in a couple of days to try and avert a few of the complications, but it seemed the babies wanted to come early.

"It— it is!" Heidi said, and squeezed her eyes closed, obviously in an immense amount of pain. "Where's Dave? I thought he was just grabbing the baby bag? Dave! Dave, you get out here right now!"

Chloe felt a little worried that Heidi's screams would alert the whole neighborhood to her condition, but nobody else seemed to be paying them any attention, and Chloe was grateful for that. Dave came flying out the door a second later, laden with bags. He looked utterly terrified and Chloe couldn't help but feel a little sympathetic for the father-to-be.

"Here I am!" he said, obviously trying to sound enthusiastic through his terror. "Just had to grab a couple of last minute things. Hi, Chloe! We'll see you at the hospital!"

Before Chloe could even say anything in response, the paramedics loaded Heidi into the ambulance as she screamed in pain. It was so scary to see her best friend in such agony, and all Chloe could do was hope they would be able to save both Heidi and the babies at the hospital.

As the ambulance pulled away with

its sirens blaring, Chloe tore down the street and back to her car. She followed right behind the ambulance all the way to the hospital, but when they got there, she unfortunately had to find parking, which delayed her. By the time she managed to find out where they'd taken Heidi on the OB/GYN floor, her friend was already hooked up to a million wires and monitors. When Chloe entered the room, Dave was holding Heidi's hand and talking to her as a doctor stood at the end of the bed, looking anxious.

"You have to finish transforming, my love," Dave whispered to Heidi, who looked very weak and pale. Chloe's heart positively ached at the sight of her. "If you're in your wolf form, you and the boys will have the best chance of

LUCIFER

survival. I know it's hard, and I know you're in so much pain right now, but please Heidi, you can do this."

As Chloe watched in awe, Heidi nodded almost imperceptibly as she continued bracing through the pain, and then she completed her transformation. Her gorgeous hair transformed into fur, her elegant nose grew out into a snout, and her delicate arms became forepaws. The moment she became a wolf, she seemed to get stronger and looked like she was in less pain. The doctor checked her.

"Good, this was just what she needed! She's at ten centimeters, everyone who isn't the father please leave the room and get me the rest of my team!"

GINA KINCADE & ERZABET BISHOP

Chloe didn't even have time to say a word before the whole room filled with people. Chloe knew she was in good hands, and although it was still very scary to leave her, she was no longer terrified that she was going to lose her best friend.

She left the room swiftly and strode down the hall to the visitor's lounge. She waited in there for the next two hours, too afraid to go back to the room on the off chance she wasn't supposed to be in there. She also wanted to give Dave and Heidi some time alone with their boys. Finally after about two and a half hours, she casually walked back down the hall, waiting for someone to tell her she shouldn't be there. When no one said a word to her, she pulled back her shoulders and acted like she knew she could be there. She knocked softly on the door and heard someone walk over right away.

Dave pulled the door open and stepped back. He looked completely exhausted but yet utterly delighted. He held a tiny bundle cradled in his arms and when he saw Chloe, he flashed her a grin and ushered her in.

"Come in, come in!" he said, his excitement palatable as he presented the first little one to Chloe. She gasped when she saw the adorable little thing all scrunched up in his blanket. "This is Ronan!"

"Oh my goodness, he's perfect!" Chloe cooed, clasping her hand over her heart and feeling a depth of love like she'd never known before for the little one immediately.

"Of course he is, I made him!" came Heidi's tired voice from the bed. Chloe looked up, elated to find her friend had transformed back into being a human already and held the other bundle of joy to her breast. The women smiled warmly at each other.

"I should have known!" Chloe said, chuckling. "So this is Ronan, and that's…"

"Romulus," Heidi said, and gestured to the nursing baby. "Two perfectly healthy boys. We don't know if they're shifters, demons or both, and we probably won't until they hit puberty. But that's fine with us, we only care that they're doing well. Romulus, he's doing so well he's barely taken a second away from eating. It seems he takes after his father!" she chuckled and flashed her husband a smile.

Chloe and Dave laughed, and then Heidi motioned for Chloe to come over to her. Chloe went to stand by her best friend's bedside.

"I'm so glad you're all right," Chloe said, gently placing her hand on her friend's cheek. "You gave us a real scare there for a while."

"I'm glad everything worked out, too," Heidi said, tilting her head into the warmth of her friend's hand. She put her hand on top of Chloe's and squeezed. "But you should have known I would be fine! I always am, aren't I?"

Both women chuckled, and then

Heidi flashed Chloe a hard look.

"Mackenzie texted me about you and Lucifer," she told her. "Why didn't you tell me?"

"She did?" Chloe said in surprise. "No, of course she did. I should have known. I— I didn't want to worry you when you had so much other stuff on your mind, Heidi. I mean, if I had, then you would probably have been giving me advice while you were in labor!"

Heidi laughed, and then looked at Chloe seriously again. "My sweet girl. While that may very well be true, I need to tell you that I think you should be with Lucifer. The two of you are perfect for each other, and you've wanted a life mate for such a long time. If today taught me anything, it's that life is too

LUCIFER

short, and far too precious to miss out on big opportunities like this. I'm not telling you what to do... I'm just suggesting you take your own advice for once and seize this opportunity by the... horns!"

Chloe laughed. "Horns? As in, because he's a demon?"

Heidi nodded. "Duh. I'm an expert pun maker." She grinned.

Both women laughed again, and then Chloe gave her friend a small, grateful smile.

"Thank you, Heidi. I've been thinking a lot about it, because it's so much to think about. But Lucifer is a wonderful man, and I know that we'll be happy together—"

"So then go! Be with him! Don't worry

about us here, we're fine!" Heidi said, shooing her out of the room. Chloe heard Dave laugh behind her and looked at both of them in turn.

"Are you sure? I want to stay around in case either of you need anything," Chloe said honestly.

"I'll handle anything she needs from here, thanks Chloe," Dave said gratefully. "And for the record... I think you should go be with Lucifer, too." He flashed her a grin.

Chloe chuckled and then looked back at Heidi. "Did you pay him to say that?"

Heidi shook her head innocently. "No, of course not! Now go, before I make one of the nurses come in here and drag you out by your ear!"

They all laughed and then Chloe bid

LUCIFER

them farewell, thanking them for their sound advice. But as she closed the door to their room, she turned down the hall and froze.

Lucifer stood at the end of the hallway with a big bouquet of flowers in one hand and a bunch of balloons in his other.

"Chloe," he said quietly, but he didn't move.

"Lucifer?" she said quizzically. "What are you doing here?"

"I'm sorry, I know you asked me to give you space," he said, and walked toward her. "But I could sense that your friend was in labor and might be in trouble. I... I just wanted to make sure you were both okay. I got these balloons for Heidi and... These are for you. I could also sense you were helping her a great deal, and I thought you deserved a gift of appreciation."

"That's so sweet of you. Oh my. Thank you! These flowers are beautiful!" Chloe felt the color rise in her cheeks and she smiled delightedly. "No, no, please don't apologize for coming here I... I was actually leaving because I needed to talk to you."

Lucifer took in a quick, worried breath, and it made Chloe's heart melt. "You did? Oh. All right, should we... should we go somewhere private?"

Chloe smiled and shook her head. She took a step toward him and wrapped her arms around his waist. "No. I can tell you all that I need to right here."

Chloe tilted her head to look up at the

shockingly handsome demon, her fated mate. She rocked forward on her heels and kissed him.

Lucifer was so surprised that he didn't move for a second, but once he realized what was happening, his eyes softened and the corners of his lips curled into a smile.

"Chloe, I hate to press, but does this mean you've made a decision?" His voice trembled with emotion. Lucifer slipped his arms around her as best as he could with all of the stuff in his hands. A muscle in his jaw twitched.

Chloe couldn't imagine being any happier than she was in this moment.

She let out a long breath and placed her hands over his heart, which thrummed beneath her touch. She let her gaze sweep up from his lips to his eyes, noting the tiniest hints of red now rimmed the edges of the whites. She stared deeply into his eyes. "Lucifer, I want to be your fated mate for all eternity. I want you to claim me, and I want to claim you in return. I have no regrets about this decision, and I think we should make this final as soon as possible!"

Lucifer's eyes widened and he grinned. He slid the pad of this thumb over her cheekbone and said in a voice thick with emotion, "Chloe, you've made me the happiest man on earth, and the happiest demon in Purgatory!"

Warmth filled her heart and spread across her chest. Chloe flung her arms around his neck and giggled. He pressed

LUCIFER

a kiss on her lips, setting her skin alight as heat filled her belly and happy tears filled her vision.

CHAPTER TWENTY-ONE

"OH MY— OH, my devil!" Chloe exclaimed the first time she went down to Purgatory and laid eyes on Lucifer's castle. "This is where you live?"

Lucifer nodded proudly and beamed at her. "It sure is. Do you like it?"

Chloe scoffed. "How could I not? This looks like something out of medieval

LUCIFER

England," she gushed, her voice breathy with awe.

The castle stood before them, with all of its silvery grey bricks covered in a gentle layer of moss and ivy. There were four turrets on the outside of the castle, and three towers jutting upward toward the sky. Unlike some of the medieval castles in England, however, this one looked very welcoming and warm. There were flowers growing in the beds just in front of the castle, the grass in front was lush and green, and ruby red curtains billowed out of many of the windows.

"I'm so glad you're happy with it," Lucifer said, wrapping his arm around her shoulders, tucking her to his side, and admiring the castle as well. "I made a few adjustments to my home and the surrounding area. I needed things to look a little less... fire and brimstone before you arrived."

Chloe laughed and wrapped her arms around Lucifer's waist, rocking up on her tiptoes to place a kiss on the corner of his mouth. When she pulled away, she looked up at him adoringly and said, "I love it almost as much as I love you!"

They both laughed and then, clasping her hand in his, Lucifer led her inside. When they entered, Chloe gasped again. Crafted of marble, the entranceway boasted shimmery ornate golden trim around the floors and ceilings. A grand staircase with an elegant, polished dark cherry wood banister cascaded down the center of the room, leading up to the next floors. Chloe felt so excited, she couldn't catch her breath. It looked beautiful.

"Shall I give you the grand tour?" Lucifer asked, his eyes twinkling.

Chloe flung her arms around his neck, pressing her body against his. "I would love nothing more than for you to show me around. But first, I want to apologize for ever doubting that this place would be beautiful."

Lucifer shook his head dismissively, his eyes softening and the corners of his lips turning up in a smile. "You have nothing to apologize for, my love. Of course you would have doubts about coming here. You'd never visited Purgatory before. And I think it might have been coupled with a concern about living both here and on earth, is that right?"

Chloe nodded shyly. "Yes, that may have been part of it. But now, I'm so happy we've figured out our time so I get to spend enough time up on earth with you, and down here, too!"

Lucifer flashed her a brilliant, mega-watt smile and slid his hand from her waist down to cup her ass. "Oh, me too, my love. Me too!" He grinned and wiggled his eyebrows suggestively.

Chloe lifted her hand to cup the side of his face, her thumb brushing over his full lips. "Lucifer, you are the most caring, wonderful, sensual man, and I'm so happy you're my soulmate. I can't wait to spend forever with you."

Lucifer flashed her the widest smile she'd ever seen him give and it made her heart flutter. "I feel the same way about you, my love. You are stunningly gorgeous, incredibly kind, and you set my heart on fire each time I look at you. I love you more than anything."

He brushed his mouth over hers, sending sparks thrumming across her nerves in a rush. Chloe could have kissed him forever.

When they finally pulled apart, Lucifer grasped Chloe's hand and pulled her to the stairs. "Come along! The tour has just begun, and as a special treat, we'll go visit the DeLux Cafe!"

Chloe paused with one foot on the stair and looked at him quizzically. "Wait. You want to go all the way back up to earth for lunch?" She cocked her head to the side the way her wolf would if she didn't understand something.

Lucifer chuckled and shook his head. "No, of course not. Don't you know the other half of the DeLux cafe, the lower part, is down here in Purgatory?"

Chloe's eyes widened. "Oh, my devil. I never realized that."

Lucifer laughed uproariously, a great loud baritone sound that sent chills skating down her spine, and eventually Chloe joined him with her own howling chortle. She couldn't believe she hadn't realized that before, but it all made sense now. As they ascended the stairs and walked into the first room, Chloe felt happier than she had in a long, long time. She finally felt like she was home in Lucifer's arms. She knew she had made the right decision, and she

LUCIFER

couldn't imagine a more perfect man... or demon... to be with than Lucifer.

***

"And that's it, the upper floor of my humble abode here in Purgatory. Of course, it contains the bedrooms so it's also the most important wing, in my personal opinion." Lucifer winked and flashed Chloe a Cheshire cat grin.

"Humble abode, my ass! It's a bloody castle, Lucifer. Even if I spend every day here for the rest of my life, I doubt I'll ever remember where every room is and that's only the top floor so far." Chloe smacked Lucifer on the arm.

"Oh my, and what an ass it is, my dearest Chloe!" Lucifer slid a hand around to cup her buttock with a squeeze.

Laughing, Chloe pressed herself flush against his body, and his hot, pulsing erection pressed back. She moaned and he swallowed the sound with a toe-curling, searing kiss.

He drew back, staring down at her though darkened eyes. "Now, you said you wanted to make this mating official as soon as possible, right? How does right now sound to you, my love?"

Her animal rubbed beneath her skin, ready to bond with their mate. He wasn't a wolf, but that didn't matter. He felt like home and despite the suddenness of it all, there was no place else she would rather be.

Chloe nodded emphatically, heat blooming through her cheeks, and the

LUCIFER

two scampered down the hall, their hands clasped tightly, matching grins plastered on their features. It only took them a few minutes to make their way back to Lucifer's enormous bedroom.

As they tumbled through the door, Lucifer kicked it closed behind them and turned to capture Chloe with a large hand around her waist, pulling her against his chest and leaning her back against the closed door, his eyes alight with lust and mischief.

"C'mere, my little wolf," he growled, his voice thick with barely restrained emotion, eyes rimmed in crimson.

"Lucifer..." She tilted her head and looked up into his glittering eyes, pressing her hands against his chest, his heart thrumming under her palm.

GINA KINCADE & ERZABET BISHOP

He captured her chin in his hands and brought his mouth to play over hers.

She slid her hands up over his chest, grasped the edges of his button down shirt, and pulled the two halves apart, baring his sculpted chest to her gaze. She cared nothing about the buttons that now littered the floor around them. Pushing her hands up over his shoulders, she tangled her fingers in his dark, silky locks and moaned deep in her throat.

Lucifer pulled his mouth from hers, his breaths coming fast and heavy. "Oh, Detective, is that how we're playing it now? Aggressive. I like it!" His crimson-rimmed eyes glowed as he ran his hands down over her breasts, one coming to rest on her hip, the other sliding down to cup her dewy, panty-covered cleft. "My turn. These need to go." He chuckled, the sound vibrating against her hardened nipples where they pressed against his chest through the thin material of her dress.

Heat exploded in her belly and additional moisture rushed to settle between her thighs as he gripped the side of her panties and tore them from her hips with one flick of his wrist. His thick fingers feathered over her bare folds, his thumb finding the swollen nubbin and circling as he moved his mouth to suckle the sensitive skin at the base of her throat.

Chloe closed her eyes and pressed her head back against the door, her breaths coming in frantic gusts. Thousands of nerve endings came alive inside her body. They spread from the point of contact to travel up her abdomen, only to begin all over again. A cry ripped from her lips as she bucked her hips and ground herself against his hand.

She couldn't breathe... think... or move for that matter. She remained suspended in her current position, chasing a feeling that seemed just out of reach.

His circling thumb grew in strength, giving her just the added pressure she needed to sail off into the abyss. She felt her core tightening, the muscles contracting and grasping on air as he worked her closer to the edge with every

LUCIFER

flick of his wrist.

"That's it," he coaxed, tightening his hold on her back. "Just let go...I got you. Come for me, Chloe," Lucifer demanded.

And then it happened.

The humming nerves that had been racing through her belly to her core suddenly ignited. Lightning exploded behind her eyes, her back arched, and a cry wrenched from her in hoarse surrender. Her entire body seized, her muscles locked up and she crested the wave of her climax as his teeth grazed the sensitive skin of her shoulder. Her release seemed to go on forever, holding her in a state of euphoria she never wanted to come back from. She tightened her hands in his hair, mewling and panting through the aftershocks of breaths coming in frantic gusts. Thousands of nerve endings came alive inside her body. They spread from the point of contact to travel up her abdomen, only to begin all over again. A cry ripped from her lips as she bucked her hips and ground herself against his hand.

She couldn't breathe... think... or move for that matter. She remained suspended in her current position, chasing a feeling that seemed just out of reach.

His circling thumb grew in strength, giving her just the added pressure she needed to sail off into the abyss. She felt her core tightening, the muscles contracting and grasping on air as he worked her closer to the edge with every

LUCIFER

flick of his wrist.

"That's it," he coaxed, tightening his hold on her back. "Just let go...I got you. Come for me, Chloe," Lucifer demanded.

And then it happened.

The humming nerves that had been racing through her belly to her core suddenly ignited. Lightning exploded behind her eyes, her back arched, and a cry wrenched from her in hoarse surrender. Her entire body seized, her muscles locked up and she crested the wave of her climax as his teeth grazed the sensitive skin of her shoulder. Her release seemed to go on forever, holding her in a state of euphoria she never wanted to come back from. She tightened her hands in his hair, mewling and panting through the aftershocks of her orgasm, half expecting her now weak legs to buckle beneath her.

"Oh, Lucifer... I... Oh my. That was..." She exhaled a shaky breath, still reeling from the intensity of her climax.

Lucifer waited for her orgasm to slow and then eased his fingers away from her sopping slit. "Hold on, baby, there's so much more where that came from." He leaned down and grasped her ass cheeks, lifting her in his arms and carrying her toward the bed. He carefully deposited her on her back in the center of the huge mattress.

Chloe stared up at him, watching his every move through a haze of desire.

Lucifer stood at the edge of the bed, staring back at her with hooded eyes. He kneeled and rested a knee on the edge of the bed, easing her legs apart once more. "So wet... So beautiful..."

Slipping his arms beneath her knees, he lifted her legs over his shoulders and settled down between her thighs.

The first touch of his tongue along her slit sent Chloe's eyes rolling back in pleasure, but nothing prepared her for the feel of his lips sucking her overly sensitive flesh into his mouth. He lashed her with his tongue without breaking the suction even as she bucked and keened, threading her fingers tightly in his dark hair once more.

Somewhere in the far reaches of her mind, Chloe became acutely aware that the rest of her clothing had somehow simply vanished. At that moment, fully bared to his gaze, amid the throbbing ache in her core, she couldn't have cared less about her fleshy jiggly bits.

"Please," she panted, begging for something... anything, though she didn't know what exactly.

Lucifer nodded, humming his appreciation into her folds, continuing the delicious onslaught of pleasure. A moan escaped her as he pressed a finger deep into her pussy. "So goddamn tight."

"Lucifer... I need..." Her breath came in gasps, her mind unable to focus on a thought, and her vaginal walls gripped his finger, seeking release.

A sexy laugh rumbled inside his chest. "You like that, beautiful?"

"Yes," she gasped, moving her hips in time with his finger. Chloe wasn't sure how long Lucifer worshiped her with his mouth, pushing her to the point of orgasm once more before releasing her and rising from between her shaking legs.

He stared down at her through glassy, unfocused eyes, his tongue flicking out to taste her essence on his glistening lips. "You taste so damn good. I have always been a fan of delicious cream." He reached for his buckle, slipping the black leather belt from the loops, his intense, crimson-clouded stare never leaving hers.

Chloe couldn't take her gaze off his hands as he reached for the remnants of his shirt and slipped it down over his broad shoulders, tossing the garment to the floor. She would never get enough of looking at his chest. His sheer size intimidated her, and the dusting of hair that ran the length of his stomach had to be one of the sexiest things she'd ever seen. Heaving an impatient sigh, she flicked her tongue out to moisten her lips. Her wolf whined, agreeing they'd waited long enough for this moment and it was taking far too long for her liking. "Lucifer, if you don't speed this up a bit I will take things into my own hands." She flashed him a lecherous grin

"Mmmm, Detective, I like the sound of that. I would happily submit myself to your hands." He grinned and flashed a brilliant, toothy grin of his own. His long masculine fingers moved to the top of his jeans, popping the button free and sliding the zipper down. Chloe held her breath as he dragged them down his muscular thighs and stepped out of them.

He climbed his way up her body, leaning on his arms and hovering above her. His delicious scent drifted up her nose, and more wetness dripped from her swollen, needy sex, preparing her for what she craved most.

"So fucking sexy," he growled, lowering his body to hers and guiding his huge, engorged shaft to her hungry entrance. "Is this what you want, my love?"

"Yes... Lucifer, yes. Take me, claim me, make me yours in all ways. Now!" Chloe growled, her pebbled nipples tightening more as they grazed against the hair on his chest. Her nails lengthened and tuffs of snow white fur burst from the skin on her arms as she fought to hold back her wolf. The feel of his mushroomed head against her opening and the scent of him invading her awareness felt incredible to her starved senses. She wrapped her legs around his waist and pulled him to her, rolling her hips as the last threads on her patience snapped, demanding she take control before she lost herself.

The feel of his thick shaft stretching her, possessing her, left Chloe in a state of bliss she never wanted to return from. Nerves came alive once again, stronger this time, and fire zinged through her veins as Lucifer flexed his broad hips with a gentle thrust, entering her completely.

Lucifer wrapped his arms around her

LUCIFER

hips, jerking her against him as he drove himself into her to the hilt again and again. He pistoned his hips, taking her higher, pushing her, demanding her surrender with every calculated stroke. He rose to his knees, lifting her with him, and swiveled his hips, grinding against her with enough pressure to work her clit along with her sweet spot into a commanding release.

"Come for me, baby. Come for me now," Lucifer growled low in his throat, never slowing the rapid, punishing movement of his hips as his skin turned crimson, his wings emerged from his back and flapped high above them, and she decided he looked even sexier with his horns protruding from his forehead.

Razor sharp, brilliant white fangs

erupted from his gums and he leaned down, his mouth covering her breast as she felt him puncture her skin. Her back arched, and her eyes rolled back in her head as she felt him suckling against her sensitive skin. She'd never known her body to be capable of such intense pleasure.

Chloe felt herself transforming and let it happen. Her mouth elongated and a fine layer of snow white fur sprouted from her skin, covering her arms, legs, and face now. She pressed her fangs to Lucifer's shoulder and bit down on him, completing the claiming process. As her teeth broke the skin and his life blood pooled in her mouth, it felt like a bomb of pleasure went off inside her.

She screamed, her back bowed off the

LUCIFER

bed as fiery heat rushed through her. The muscles of her throbbing core clamped down on his cock, milking him of his own orgasm as he threw back his head and roared, powerful jets of his scorching seed expelling from his body, coating her insides.

They'd come together as they never had before, and two fated mates became one, united for all eternity.

He dropped down over her, his hips continuing to jerk in short, quick bursts, his tongue flicking out to trace over the puncture marks on her breast, his saliva sealing the still trickling dual perforations.

She buried her face against his neck, inhaling the sensually masculine smoky burnt cinnamon scent that was Lucifer.

"That was amazing."

Lifting his head, Lucifer studied her face for a moment before gently pulling his still hard cock from her body. "Are you in any pain?"

Chloe shook her head and smiled up at her soulmate. "I'm a little tender, but the pleasure far outweighs any pain I felt."

"I love you, Chloe Frost," Lucifer said, looking down at her with such adoration in his eyes Chloe thought she might actually explode. Emotion surged in her heart, filling it to bursting.

"I love you, too, Lucifer Morningstar," Chloe whispered.

EPILOGUE

"GOOD MORNING, YOU two!" Hera greeted Chloe and Lucifer at the Butternut bakery a month later. "Demi, the King and Queen of Darkness are here!"

"You know that you don't have to call us that, right, Hera?" Chloe grinned. "You can just call us by our names.

LUCIFER

"Oh, I know, I know," the goddess said, preparing them their usual orders. "But when you're walking down the street every person in Purgatory bows to you, so I feel like I have to do a little something, ya know?" Hera grinned.

Everyone laughed, and then Demi appeared from behind the curtain just to the right of the counter.

"Your Highnesses!" she said, bowing to them. "How wonderful to see you. Chloe, how are you feeling?"

Chloe smiled warmly at Demi and squeezed Lucifer's hand while he beamed at her. "Pretty well, thank you. The worst of the morning sickness seems to have passed, thanks to Hera's special herbal tonic, and none too soon, I might add. Kneeling in front of a porcelain throne isn't my preferred choice, if you know what I mean." Chloe winked, heat blooming in her cheeks.

"Oh, I'm so relieved to hear that," Hera said, handing Chloe her decaf tea and Lucifer his black coffee. "We wouldn't want our Queen to suffer any more than she has to!"

Lucifer and Chloe bid the owners of the bakery farewell amid their thank yous, and then returned to the quaint street. Purgatory looked a lot brighter and prettier now that Chloe lived here part time. Lucifer's joy was reflected in the ever-blooming flowers that hung from the lampposts, the rainbows that streamed across the sky after it rained, and the way the crumbling buildings were being fixed up by the locals. As they walked down the street now, Chloe couldn't have imagined a more perfect town to spend half of her time in.

"Do you think they already know?" Chloe said, tenderly touching her stomach. She took a sip of her decaf coffee and hummed her appreciation.

Lucifer shook his head from side-to-side. "I think there's a pretty good chance they've figured out that we're getting married, but I don't think even Heidi could guess that you're pregnant. You aren't showing at all yet." He winked.

Chloe grinned, a chuckle slipping from her throat, and then she and Lucifer chatted idly as they walked around to the back of the Butternut Bakery where the patio was. They were meeting Heidi, Dave, Ronan and Romulus for lunch. When they walked through the gate, Chloe was happy to see their friends were already there sitting at the table. When Heidi saw Chloe, she jumped up, ran to her and enveloped her in a big hug.

"Chloe!" she cried happily. "Oh, it's so good to see you! It's been so—"

But Heidi suddenly froze. Chloe pulled away from her to see what the problem was.

"Are you okay?" Chloe asked as she saw the concerned look on her friend's face.

Heidi gave Chloe a hard look. "Excuse me. Why didn't you tell me that you were pregnant?"

Chloe's eyes widened and she looked

back at Lucifer, who shared the same shocked look. "H-how did you— How did you know?"

Heidi shot Chloe an unimpressed look. "Honey, I could smell it on you from a mile away, even though I'm not in my wolf form."

There was a beat, and then both women giggled. "I'm only two months along, so we're trying to keep it quiet, and I was going to tell you today."

Heidi squealed with delight and hugged her friend again. "Oh I'm so happy for you! But this must mean... this has to mean..."

Chloe nodded to her friend and showed her the engagement ring on her finger. Heidi looked like she was about to die with happiness. She grasped Chloe by the arms and screamed, "My best friend is getting married!"

Heidi then hugged her so tightly that Chloe thought she was going to burst. Finally, Heidi let her go and Chloe and Lucifer followed Heidi over to the table to begin discussing the details of their wedding with their two closest friends. They had decided to be married in a hurry, as Chloe would be showing soon, so they only had a few months to plan. But Heidi and Dave couldn't have been happier for them, and they promised to do everything they could to help.

As they ate their lunch and talked wedding and babies, Lucifer and Dave gushed over Ronan and Romulus, taking care of them the whole time. It made Chloe's heart grow three sizes to see her

LUCIFER

King of the Underworld holding little Ronan so tenderly in his arms and feeding him a bottle. She knew she had made the right decision with him, and didn't ever want to leave his side again.

As Chloe sat at the table at the Butternut Cafe discussing all of their exciting news with her best friends and her fiancée, she looked around in awe. Had she imagined this perfect life a few months ago, she wouldn't have believed it even possible. She took a moment to close her eyes and connect with her white wolf.

We did it girl. We found our soulmate.

Her wolf chuffed and gave a happy yip.

All felt right in the world now and Chloe couldn't help but think her future looked amazing.

Her wolf barked her agreement and Chloe grinned.

Thank you for reading!

If you enjoyed Lucifer, please return to the retailer where you made your purchase and leave a review. Even a few short words may make an author's day and encourage them to keep writing.

Watch your favorite online retailer for the other books in the Speed Dating with the Denizens of the Underworld series.

Turn the page now for an excerpt from *Ash by C.D. Gorri*, Book Two in the Speed Dating with the Denizens of the Underworld series!

EXCERPT

From Sunday school teacher to Werewolf and mate in under forty-eight hours. Speed dating sure is fast in this steamy Underworld romance.

Speed dating.

Her?

What was Mim thinking?

LUCIFER

It was almost as unbelievable to conceive of as the notion that she, Gabriella Keen, Sunday school teacher and all around goody two shoes, was a Werewolf.

You are a Wolf.

Grrr.

She stopped midstep and closed her eyes, trying to get her growling bits, as in her Wolf and her stomach both, to shut the flub up.

Sigh.

She really needed to start cursing. But dang it, she just couldn't. The f word turned into all sorts of silly things like *funk*, *flub*, *flap*, and *furp*. The s word often became *shoot*, the b word stopped at *bit*, and so on.

"Gabby, right? Look, dear, the rest is

all easy to follow. You sit, drink, chat, sniff, see if you click. And if you don't, just move on when the timer dings."

"Wait, what? Sniff? Ding? Huh?" Gabby's eyebrows disappeared into her hairline. She inhaled a breath, then another, trying not to hyperventilate with this new and sudden influx of information.

"I'm sorry, I meant no offence," Aphrodite replied, looking properly chided. Heck. This woman had pouting down to an art.

"I tend to forget my manners sometimes, but honestly, Wolves and other Shifters tend to sniff out their mates. Something about the Fates lacing their pheromones with something that triggers awareness when their destined mate is near."

"Look, I don't know what is happening here. Is this real? Was Mim serious? And are you really leading me to some underground speed dating thing?"

"Honey, I gather you haven't *changed* yet, is that right?"

"But I did change my dress—"

"Not your dress," Aphrodite whispered, taking her by the arm and pulling her down the last few steps.

She stopped her just on the other side of the polished staircase, in a dark secluded corner. Gabriella was breathing heavily. There were too many fragrances assaulting her senses, and her stomach tightened as she started to panic, albeit mildly.

"Look at me, Gabriella," Aphrodite commanded. "I am sure Mariah meant well, throwing you in the deep end like this, but I have one question for you before you begin."

Gabby nodded, willing the woman to just get on with it already.

What did she want to know?

Did insanity run in the family?

Had she gotten her flea shots?

Was she gonna potty on the floor?

Chew on the chairs?

What, dang it, what?!

"Are you a virgin?"

Well, that wasn't what she'd expected. Gabby stopped hyperventilating and straightened her shoulders. Her cheeks burned, and she knew they'd be a dusky, unflattering

LUCIFER

shade of pink that clashed with the red lights of the room they were now in.

"Hey, I may not look like you, oh Goddess of love, but I have been in love. At least, I thought I'd been. And the answer is no, I am not a virgin."

"Great! I was worried for a minute. Follow me," Aphrodite replied with an even wider grin than before. "Welcome," she said, indicating the room before her, "to Speed Dating With the Denizens of the Underworld!"

Snag your copy of Ash at your favorite online retailer!

Watch for the other books in the Speed Dating with the Denizens of the Underworld Series

Lucifer
Ash
Azrael
Azazel
Samael
Hecate
Bastet
Cain
Thor
Demi
Hell's Belle
Arachne
Osiris
Hades
Adam
Loki

LUCIFER

Lilith

The Morrígan

Orion

Hera

Abel

Odin

Mormos

Zeus

Michael

Váli

Apollo

Raphael

Baldur

Poseidon

Gabrielle

Frigg

Uriel

And More!

MORE FROM GINA KINCADE

Shadow Legacies

Hunter Moon

Ghost Moon

Blood Moon

Coming Soon!

LUCIFER

Born of Hellfire

Hellbound Heart

Demon's Playground

Devil's Mate

Coming Soon!

Shifting Hearts Dating App

Mistle Tie Me

Bear It All

Chocolate Moon Cafe

Your Wolfish Heart

Outfoxing Her Mate

Shifting Hearts Dating App: Books 1-3

Shifting Hearts Dating Agency

One True Mate: Furever Shifter Mates, Book 2

His Furever Mate: Furever Shifter Mates, Book 3

Coming Soon!

Green Rock Falls

Accidentally Forever

Single Titles

What Lies Within Us

A Modern Day Witch Hunt

When the Snow Flies

CONNECT WITH GINA

Facebook

https://www.facebook.com/authorginakincade

Newsletter Mailing List

https://landing.mailerlite.com/webforms/landing/r1r5n4

Amazon

https://www.amazon.com/Gina-Kincade/e/B00WSRLHVO/

Twitter

https://twitter.com/ginakincade

BookBub

https://www.bookbub.com/authors/gina-kincade

Blog/Webpage:

https://www.ginakincade.com

Instagram

https://www.instagram.com/ginakincade

Goodreads

https://www.goodreads.com/ginakincade

ABOUT GINA KINCADE

USA Today Bestselling Author Gina Kincade spends her days tapping away at a keyboard, through blood, sweat, and often many tears, crafting steamy paranormal romances filled with shifters and vampires, along with witchy urban fantasy tales in magical worlds she hopes her readers yearn to crawl into.

LUCIFER

A busy mom of three, she loves healthy home cooking, gardening, warm beaches, fast cars, and horseback riding.

Ms. Kincade's life is full, time is never on her side, and she wouldn't change a moment of it!

Find more from Gina at: https://www.ginakincade.com/

WHERE TO FIND MORE OF ERZABET BISHOP

Amazon

https://www.amazon.com/Erzabet-Bishop/e/B00AVSDUBC

Twitter

@erzabetbishop.

Instagram

https://www.instagram.com/erzabetbishop/

LUCIFER

Bookbub

https://www.bookbub.com/authors/erzabet-bishop

Website and Newsletter

http://erzabetwrites.wix.com/erzabetbishop

Facebook Author Page

https://www.facebook.com/erzabetbishopauthor

Goodreads

http://www.goodreads.com/author/show/6590718.Erzabet_Bishop

ALSO BY ERZABET BISHOP

Shadow Legacies

Hunter Moon

Ghost Moon

Blood Moon

Coming Soon!

LUCIFER

Born of Hellfire

Hellbound Heart

Demon's Playground

Devil's Mate

Coming Soon!

Shifting Hearts Dating Agency Series

Hedging Her Bets

Waking Up Wolf

Kitten Around

Shifting Hearts Dating Agency Collection Books 1-3

Shifting Hearts Dating App Series

Mistle Tie Me

GINA KINCADE & ERZABET BISHOP

Your Wolfish Heart

Chocolate Moon Cafe

Bear It All

Outfoxing Her Mate

Shifting Hearts Dating App: Books 1-3

My Wicked Mates Series

Craving Her Mates

Surrendering to Her Mate

Tormenting Her Mate

My Wicked Mates Series Collection: Books 1-3

Westmore Wolves Series

Wicked for You

Heart's Protector

Burning for You

LUCIFER

Taming the Beast

Mistletoe Kisses

Westmore Wolves Collection, Books 1-5

Curse Workers Series

Sanguine Shadows

Map of Bones

Malediction

Arcane

Curse Workers Collection: Books 1-3

Sigil Fire Series

Sigil Fire

Written on Skin

Glitter Lust

First Christmas: A Sigil Fire Holiday Romance

GINA KINCADE & ERZABET BISHOP

Collections and Anthologies

Holidays and More:
A Lesfic Short Story Collection

Lesfic Tales:
A Lesfic Short Story Collection

Sapphic Holiday Cruise:
A Lesbian Holiday Collection

Sweet Sensations:
A Short Story Anthology

Standalone Novels

Snow

ABOUT ERZABET BISHOP

ERZABET BISHOP IS A USA TODAY BESTSELLING and award-winning author of over forty paranormal and contemporary romance books. She lives in Houston, Texas, and when she isn't writing about sexy shifters or voluptuous heroines, she enjoys playing in local bookstores and watching movies with her husband and furry kids.

LUCIFER

Printed in Great Britain
by Amazon